by Ethel Calvert Phillips

Cover design by Phillip Colhouer
Original illustrations by Maginel Wright Barney
Cover illustration by Dan Burr
Inside illustrations recreated by Milena and Jelena Vitorovic
This unabridged version has updated grammar and spelling.
First published in 1932
Originally titled *Pyxie: A Little Boy of the Pines*

www.thegoodandthebeautiful.com

Table of Contents

1. The Piney Boy 1

2. Amanda. 11

3. The New Home 20

4. The First Day at School 30

5. The Green Van 40

6. The Book Lady 49

7. Miss Grant Asks a Question. 57

8. A Surprise for Miss Bird 66

9. A Day's Ride 75

10. Daniel Boone. 84

11. The Cranberry Pickers 98

12. Forest Fire 110

13. The Story That Miss Bird Told 122

Chapter 1

The Piney Boy

"Boy, what you doing with all those leaves?"

"What you want to know for?" was the boy's reply.

He stood, a shabby little figure in overalls, his arms filled with dry leaves and sprays of pine needles, and he eyed with an unfriendly air the little girl who asked the question of him. A small, plump boy was clinging to her hand, and the round, black eyes of the pair were fixed in lively curiosity upon the boy and his load.

He was a thin little boy, with eyes as brown as the nearby brook, a short snub nose well sprinkled with freckles, and a shock of yellow hair that stood out around his head in untidy fashion. He wore a pair of overalls that needed a patch on either knee, and his blouse was ragged and thin.

"Are you going to build a burnfire?" questioned the little girl again. "My mother won't let me build a burnfire, not unless my father is right nearby."

"'Tain't a burnfire," muttered the boy, carefully placing his armful under a tree in a hollow already half-filled with leaves. "It's a bed."

"A bed?" The little girl looked as if she couldn't believe her ears. It must be a joke. She almost laughed. "Whose bed?"

"Mine," answered the boy defiantly. "It's my bed, and I'm going to sleep in it tonight."

"Are you mad at your folks? Have you run away from home?" The little girl looked pleased at this idea. Her bright, black eyes sparkled, and the red ribbon on top of her head seemed to stand more gaily erect.

But the boy shook his head.

"I haven't any folks," was his answer. "They've all gone away."

"And left you all alone? Tell me about it, do."

The little girl carefully placed on the ground a small basket filled with pink-and-white spring flowers and seated her brother with a thump at her side under a tree.

"Don't you dare go to sleep, Thanny Barr," she warned, giving him a few sisterly twitches and straightening his cap. "I shan't carry you home if you do. Now go on, boy. Tell why you are going to sleep out here in the woods."

"I can't stop," objected the boy in a sudden fit of shyness. "I've got to get more leaves."

But instead of going on with his work, he stood still and stared down at his companions who had come upon him unexpectedly among the pines, where he had felt himself well hidden and safe from curious eyes.

It was pleasant in the woods, the pine woods of southern New Jersey, that mild and sunny afternoon. Above the trees, swaying and murmuring in the wind, lazy little white clouds moved across a soft spring sky. In and out of the scrub oak bushes and trees, up among the pine boughs, fluttered the birds, busy now with nest-building and housekeeping cares. There were many birds—speckled brown thrushes, shy little wrens, bold robins, catbirds, and a song sparrow here and there. Over the sandy, pine-strewn ground, pointing through the tree trunks like long fingers, stretched the sunlight in slender yellow bars.

It was quiet in the woods, very quiet. The only sounds were the sighing of the pine trees, the call of the birds, and in the distance, the song of the brook, high now from the spring rains, as it rushed foaming over stones and pebbles on its way to the river below.

The silence was broken by the voice of the little girl.

"What's your name?" she was asking frankly. "My name is Amanda, Amanda Barr. And this is my brother Nathan, only we call him Thanny for short."

The boy hesitated a moment and then spoke out.

"My name is Pyxie, just Pyxie," he said.

Amanda stared for an instant and then permitted herself a little smile.

"Pyxie isn't a boy's name," she said decidedly. "Pyxie is the name of a flower, pyxie moss. There it is in my basket. I've just picked it down by the brook. It comes every spring."

And Amanda pointed to the basket of pink-and-white flowers standing at her feet.

The boy answered with an impatient shake of his head.

"I know about them," he said. "That's where my name comes from. Jenny called me Pyxie because of the pyxie moss."

"Who is Jenny? Oh! The woman you lived with? Why did she name you that? Tell me about it."

Amanda's interest was so real that Pyxie, forgetting his shyness, yielded, and dropping his armful of leaves sat down at her side. He was glad to talk to someone, even to a stranger and a girl at that. For, just now, in spite of his brave air, Pyxie was feeling rather lonely and forlorn.

"Jenny named me Pyxie after the pyxie moss," he began, with Amanda's bright eyes fixed on his face, "because one night, when the pyxie moss was all in bloom, like it is now, Jenny heard a noise at the door. And when she opened it, there I was a-lying on the doorstep, a baby, all wrapped up in somebody's old coat."

"Someone had left you there," interpreted Amanda, eagerly leaning forward. "Go on, do."

"There isn't any more to tell," said Pyxie. "I just lived there with Jenny and the menfolks until yesterday when they all moved away."

"Where did they go?" demanded Amanda. "Why didn't they take you too?"

"They wouldn't take me," was Pyxie's reply. "The menfolks didn't like me 'round."

A baby, all wrapped up in somebody's old coat

"Why didn't they like you?" interrupted Amanda.

Pyxie shook his head. "They never wanted Jenny to keep me. They didn't like children, Jenny said. But Jenny liked me, and she wouldn't have left me if the menfolks hadn't made her. They've moved far off, and they wouldn't let me come."

As Pyxie spoke, he could almost see Jenny standing before him—pretty, gypsy-like Jenny with her smile and a bit of bright green scarf tied over her flying black hair.

"I wish I was home again with Jenny," he thought. "We had good times together."

Pyxie was remembering with longing his old home, though it had been only a tumbledown little gray house, shadowed by pines, on the lonely back road, not far from where he now stood. He was recalling, too, the days—long, happy days—of wandering with Jenny in the woods, picking arbutus or pyxie moss, hunting for berries, or lying half asleep under the pines in the sun.

But the little girl was speaking again.

"Did they leave you all alone, with nobody to take care of you?"

Warm-hearted Amanda's eyes snapped with indignation. That was no way to do, to treat a boy so.

"No, they didn't leave me all alone," was Pyxie's reply. "They left me with Old Bill and his folks, up the road a piece."

"Why aren't you there now?" asked Amanda, naturally enough. "What makes you want to sleep in the woods tonight?"

"I don't want to stay with them." Pyxie shut his lips tight. "They fight, and they were going to hire me out to work on a farm, they said. So I ran away. I'd rather stay in the woods alone. That's why I was making a bed to sleep in tonight."

Amanda's look of indignation changed to one of mingled pity and doubt. It might be all very well to run away in the daytime, but it would be a different matter to stay alone in the woods at night.

Deep in his heart, Pyxie was beginning to think so, too. He felt very small and lonely as he sat sifting the pine needles through his hands.

"I wish Jenny was back," he thought. "I want my supper. I want to go home. But I won't go back to Old Bill's. No, I won't!"

"You can't stay here alone." Amanda had been thinking it over. "S'pose it came on to rain. And it's cold after dark, too. Where you going to get your supper tonight?"

Pyxie stared at the ground and didn't answer. He knew he wouldn't have any supper, but he didn't want to tell this strange girl so.

But already Amanda had thought of a plan.

"I'll tell you what to do," she said, her black eyes fixed on Pyxie's face. "You come home with me." She stood up as if to go at once. "My mother and my father will tell you what to do and where to stay."

Pyxie shook his head.

"I can't," he said unwillingly. "I have to stay here."

"Do you want to starve and freeze and maybe have that old man come and catch you?" Amanda almost stamped her foot. "Why can't you come home with me?"

"I like it here," muttered Pyxie, turning his face away. "I like it here in the woods. And I don't know your folks. They might do me some harm."

At this rude speech, Amanda drew herself up, her back very straight and her face growing red.

"My mother and my father won't harm you," she said stiffly. "They don't hurt people. They'll help you. They'll tell you what to do. I guess you'll be sorry if you stay here tonight."

Pyxie was ready now to believe that Amanda was right. As the hour of sunset drew near, there was a chill in the air that made him shiver in his thin blouse. He was hungry, too, very hungry. He had eaten nothing since the night before. And even then, that first unhappy night in Old Bill's house, he had been so homesick and forlorn that he scarcely had been able to swallow a mouthful. He knew he would have nothing for supper tonight but water from the brook. It had been his breakfast and his midday meal as well.

But, above all, Pyxie dreaded to be left alone. This little girl was so friendly and so sure. He did not want to let her out of his sight. She did not seem like other strangers. He was not afraid of her.

"It's late," Amanda was saying in a warning tone. "It must be 'most suppertime now."

At the mention of the word 'supper,' little Thanny scrambled to his feet. He had been so quiet, playing among the leaves, that he had been almost forgotten by the other two children.

"Come on, Amanda," urged Thanny in a plaintive voice, pulling at her dress. "I'm hungry. Come on home."

"I shouldn't wonder if you could come back here tomorrow if you like," said Amanda with a glance at Pyxie. She picked up her basket and took Thanny's hand in hers. "You coming?" She was ready to go.

Suddenly, Pyxie made up his mind. No, he couldn't let this new-found friend leave him here all alone. He knew very well how black and strange the woods could be at night. And he would have only the murmur of the pines and the song of the brook to keep him company.

"Go on. I'm coming," said Pyxie gruffly, already on his feet.

With a satisfied nod that made her red hair ribbon quiver, Amanda led the procession out of the woods.

But when they reached the narrow, sandy back road, she halted. She wanted to ask a question, unthought of until now.

"Are you a 'Piney boy'?" asked Amanda bluntly.

Pyxie stared at her, and his face grew red. Dimly he felt the reproach that lay behind her words.

"'Piney folks' are queer, living 'way back in the woods the way they do," went on outspoken Amanda. "My mother told me so. They don't want any schools or churches, and they don't go to work. They are afraid of strangers, too. My mother said 'Piney folks' were queer."

For a moment, Pyxie stood tongue-tied.

But he was thinking quickly. "If I'm a 'Piney,' they won't want me at her house."

And filled with shyness and the old fear of strangers, Pyxie turned to run.

Over his shoulder, he answered Amanda's question.

"Jenny and the menfolks are 'Pineys,'" said Pyxie, "so I guess I'm a 'Piney,' too. I'm going back."

And if Amanda had not caught his arm, he would have slipped through the bushes into the woods.

"No!" cried Amanda, holding him fast and giving his arm a little warm-hearted shake. "No! You mustn't! You come on home with me, Pyxie. I don't care one bit if you are a 'Piney boy.'"

Chapter 2

Amanda

Amanda led the way along the road with Thanny trotting at her heels and Pyxie slowly bringing up the rear. They had reached the main highway where Amanda's house stood, now only a short walk away, and every step took them farther from Old Bill and from Pyxie's former home on the lonely, untraveled back road.

Amanda was not satisfied to have Pyxie so far from her side. She felt that at any moment he might slip back among the bushes and trees and vanish. She kept a careful eye upon him, and every now and then she waited for him to catch up with her or called him near.

"Come walk right by me, Pyxie," directed Amanda. "Stay right by me."

Amanda led the way.

Silently Pyxie obeyed her bidding. But presently he slipped back into his old place. He liked it better to walk alone. It was hard for him to feel at home with strangers, even with this friendly little girl.

As they moved steadily along, Amanda, at the head of the line, had the appearance of a captain leading his army. She called out orders like a captain, too.

"Pyxie, you stay by me. Thanny, watch out for this car coming. Both of you keep up in the grass."

But Amanda was busy with her own thoughts as well as with the safety and behavior of her charges.

"I don't know what Mother will say to me," she was thinking, somewhat uneasily. "Maybe she won't like my bringing Pyxie home. But I don't believe she would have left him out in the woods all night. I'll tell her he can have my supper. He can have my bed, too, and I'll sleep on the floor."

And Amanda went over in her mind the speech she would make to her mother, down to the very last word.

When they reached home and turned in at the path, Amanda stepped back for a hasty whisper to her new-found friend.

"You stay down here," advised Amanda, "while I go up to the house and tell about you. When it's the right time, I'll call you to come in."

Amanda's father was sitting on the steps, his day's work done. Mrs. Barr, at the sound of voices, came out from the kitchen, her pleasant face red from bending over the stove.

"What's all this, Amanda?" began Mrs. Barr briskly as the little girl came up the path and halted at the foot of the steps. "Where did you pick up that child? I never saw him before. Speak out! I can't hear a word you say."

"He's a 'Piney boy,'" began Amanda in a low voice, with a backward jerk of her head. "We met him in the woods just now. He hasn't anybody to take care of him, not a one."

"Where's his folks?" interrupted her mother.

"The people he lived with moved off somewhere," said Amanda, "and left him with a horrid old man. So he ran away and was going to live in the woods and sleep on leaves for a bed."

"A boy shouldn't run away like that," said Mrs. Barr severely. "The best thing for him to do is to turn right 'round and run back again where he belongs."

And Amanda's mother looked with disapproval at Pyxie standing at the end of the path, shyly digging a hole in the dirt with his toes.

"He can't go back!" exclaimed Amanda in an indignant whisper. The scarlet hair ribbon trembled with feeling as she spoke. "They were fighting people, and they were going to hire him out to work. He's hungry. He hasn't had a bite to eat. I'll give him my supper, Mother. And if you let him stay, he can have my bed, and I'll sleep on the floor."

Amanda spoke earnestly. She meant every word she said. The speech she had planned was forgotten in the lively fear that her mother might send Pyxie away.

Mr. Barr, with Thanny on his knee, was studying the forlorn, tired little figure in his ragged overalls waiting patiently at the end of the path. Pyxie was "about beat out," as he himself would have said. And no wonder, with all that had happened to him within the past two days.

Amanda saw that her father's look was kindly, so she turned to him with her appeal. She knew, too, that her father was prone to laugh at her pranks and overlook her misdeeds. It might be he would take her part now. At least she could try.

"He's hungry," repeated Amanda pitifully. "He's hungry, Father. He hasn't had a bite to eat."

But already Mrs. Barr's motherly heart was touched by the boy's plight, and she answered before Mr. Barr could speak.

"Of course, if the child's hungry, I'll give him his supper and welcome," said Mrs. Barr warmly. "But he must belong to somebody, Amanda. You can see that. He ought to go home."

"I tell you he hasn't any home—" began Amanda. But she stopped, for her father was beckoning Pyxie to come forward.

"Let's hear what he has to say, Mother," said Mr. Barr in his slow, easy-going way. "Come up here, sonny, and tell us what you told Amanda in the woods."

Pyxie, too tired and hungry to be shy, stood at the foot of the steps and repeated his tale. And as he talked, good Mrs. Barr's face expressed all the pity that she felt for the child, and her disapproval, too, of "those shiftless Pineys," as she called them in her thoughts.

Now and then Mr. Barr asked a question.

"Where were you going to be hired out? What farm?" he said.

"I don't know," answered Pyxie. "They didn't tell. Dominick has a strawberry farm near Old Bill's, and there's another man named Tony grows vegetables down the road a ways."

"Where did your folks move to?" inquired Mr. Barr. "Won't they be coming back after a while?"

Pyxie shook his head.

"They've gone 'way off," he said with a wave of his arm. "They said they wouldn't come back, ever."

Pyxie turned his face away. He shut his lips tight so that he wouldn't cry.

"Jenny didn't want to go. Jenny liked me," he was thinking.

Mrs. Barr saw the trembling lips as she looked from plump, rosy Thanny, safe in his father's arms, to this poor little lad, left alone in the world to shift for himself. And stepping down to the path, she took the boy's hand in hers.

"You stay with us here, tonight, Pyxie," she said as gently as if she were talking to Thanny himself. "Now you go

’round to the back door with Amanda and wash yourself at the pump. Thanny, you go, too. By that time supper will be on the table. After supper, Father and I will have a talk, and then we’ll see.”

Pyxie ate his supper as if famished. He was awkward and silent and shy. He spoke only in answer to questions, and he scarcely lifted his eyes from the table.

But Mr. Barr, keeping Pyxie’s plate well filled, saw that the little brown face wore an honest look, and Mrs. Barr, from behind the teapot, caught the quick smile he unexpectedly gave her when Thanny was found eating his porridge with two spoons.

She saw, too, that his head nodded, and his eyelids drooped.

“You’re tuckered out,” said Mrs. Barr when supper was over. “Bed is the best place for you.”

So, after a bath out in the woodshed, tired Pyxie was tucked into a bed made up on the sofa, where he fell asleep almost before his head touched the pillow.

Shortly after, Amanda, half disappointed that she was not to sleep on the floor, and drowsy Thanny, nodding over his father’s shoulder, were bundled off to their own beds.

And when quiet had settled upon the household, Mr. and Mrs. Barr sat down to talk about Pyxie and what should be done.

The next morning, early, before breakfast was on the table, Amanda waylaid her mother alone in the kitchen.

“Did you talk about Pyxie last night?” she questioned eagerly. “Won’t you tell me what you’re going to do?”

"By and by I'll tell you," was her mother's prudent answer. "By and by you'll know, when the right time comes."

"Couldn't you tell me now?" inquired Amanda, with a wistful face. "I brought Pyxie here. I brought him home from the woods. I won't say a word to a single soul. I promise I won't."

Amanda wore such a beseeching air, as she laid an imploring hand on her mother's arm, that Mrs. Barr yielded and spoke.

"Don't you say a word," she began, while Amanda held her breath for fear her mother might change her mind, "but last night, after I had talked with Father, I stepped down the road to see Miss Mattie Earl."

Amanda nodded. Miss Mattie Earl was an old neighbor and friend.

"There she is, all alone in that house of hers," went on Mrs. Barr, sinking into a chair, to Amanda's delight, as if settling for a good long talk. "She is all alone, with not a soul to speak to, day in, day out. Nobody to keep her company but that ugly old gander she is so fond of, and he is out back, in a pen. So I thought to myself, in a flash, she might be glad to take Pyxie in to live with her. A 'home child' they call them, when the county pays their board."

Amanda nodded again. Her eyes were very bright. A home for Pyxie, and nearby, too!

"Does Miss Mattie want him?" she asked quickly. "When will he go? Can't I be the one to take him down to Miss Mattie's? I brought him home from the woods."

Amanda's mother shook her head at the idea of such haste.

"Why, Amanda," she said reprovingly, "Miss Mattie hasn't even seen Pyxie yet. Perhaps she won't want him at all. Maybe he has a family somewhere, too, that will have to take him back. There are things to look into, child. We must all go slow."

"Yes, ma'am." Amanda's face fell. Perhaps Pyxie would have to go back to live with Old Bill, after all.

But she felt more hopeful when her mother spoke again.

"Miss Mattie will be up here this morning to look Pyxie over," went on her mother, with a pleased air. "She liked the idea of taking a 'home child' first-rate. Now, Amanda, don't you look knowing when she walks in today, nor let one word fall. Do you hear?"

"I won't," promised Amanda earnestly. "I truly won't. But, Mother, does Miss Mattie know that Pyxie is a 'Piney boy'?"

"Yes, she does. I told her the first thing," answered Mrs. Barr, rising to her feet. "And she doesn't mind one bit. She says there is a difference in 'Pineys' and that some of them turn out a real credit to their friends. Now, Amanda, you fill the kettle. It's late. We've got to do some tall stepping 'round."

"Yes, ma'am." Amanda caught up the kettle and started out toward the pump. In the doorway she turned.

"Maybe Pyxie will be a credit," said Amanda. "And if he is, won't we all be glad that I brought him home from the woods?"

Chapter 3

The New Home

Pyxie lay in bed in Miss Mattie Earl's house, in the little white room that was now all his own. Miss Mattie Earl had said so, and surely she should know. For Pyxie now lived with Miss Mattie. He was her "home boy," she said.

It had taken some time to turn Pyxie, the "Piney boy," hungry, forlorn, without friends or shelter, into Pyxie, the "home child," now watched over by the county in which he lived and boarded by them with Miss Mattie Earl, who already had grown fond of her shy, awkward little charge.

To bring about this change, there had been more than one trip to the county seat, taken by Mr. Barr and Miss Mattie and Pyxie himself. Strangers had looked him over and talked about him and asked him many questions, more than he could answer, as it proved.

One day, Pyxie, seated between Mr. Barr and one of his new county friends, had ridden back among the pines to the house where Old Bill lived and from which Pyxie had run away. The little boy, holding fast to Mr. Barr's sleeve, had tried to hide behind this friendly arm.

"If they are going to leave me here with Old Bill," thought Pyxie in dread, "I'll run away again. I will! But I don't know how I'll get along without Miss Mattie and Amanda and Mr. and Mrs. Barr."

The narrow, sandy road, winding through the pine woods, was very familiar to Pyxie. He had walked its length with Jenny more than once. He had wandered in the woods and played in the brook more often than he could tell.

There, by the roadside, was the forlorn, tumbledown little gray house where Pyxie had lived with Jenny and her menfolks. He pointed it out to Mr. Barr and his county friend. It stood deserted now. The sagging door hung ajar and creaked slowly back and forth when the wind blew. The house was empty. Jenny and the menfolks had not come back.

Now the car jolted on, nearer and nearer to the house where Old Bill lived. Pyxie grew more frightened.

"I wish I hadn't come," he thought. "I wish I could jump out and run away."

But Mr. Barr was kind. He seemed to know how Pyxie felt. He held the little boy's hand tight in his as the car stopped before the door.

Old Bill's dogs, yelping, rushed forward. They were fierce and wild, leaping and snapping and quarreling among themselves. Faces could be seen peering from the windows and from behind the half-open door.

Old Bill himself, indifferent to Pyxie's fate, proved willing to answer a question or two.

"This boy Pyxie, that run away, no, his folks ain't ever coming back," he said with a shake of his head. "No, they ain't really his folks. He don't belong to anybody at all."

Then, abruptly, Old Bill turned his back on the car and walked away out of sight around the corner of the house.

They waited until it was plain he did not mean to come back. Then Pyxie's county friend started the car toward home. There was nothing more to be said or done here.

Presently he looked down into Pyxie's anxious little face.

"You shan't go back there to live," he said with a smile. "Never!"

And at those words, Pyxie's throat, that had been shut tight, began to feel better. He could breathe now without choking. The color came back into his cheeks. He held up his head and looked about him.

How blue the far-away sky seemed, and how clear! The pines smelled spicy and sweet in the warm sun. The birds were flying high and calling to one another with sharp, shrill cries.

Pyxie's spirits rose with every turn of the wheels. He felt lighthearted and gay. He wanted to laugh aloud.

As he passed his old home, he turned and looked back.

"There is where Jenny used to sit," he thought, gazing at the doorway and the broken steps, and recalling Jenny, with her smile for Pyxie, her red cheeks, and the bit of bright green scarf tied over her hair.

But the doorway was empty. The car rolled steadily and swiftly on. It was carrying Pyxie into a new life, very different from the old, where he would live with gentle Miss Mattie and play with Amanda and go to school.

Now Pyxie was lying in his own room—a bare, clean, white little room—that Miss Mattie had made ready for him with her own hands.

The floor was scrubbed until it shone. A strip of gay carpet lay beside the white iron bed. There was a chest of drawers, with a tiny mirror hanging over it, and beside it a small wooden chair.

The big clock in the kitchen struck six, and Miss Mattie opened the door of Pyxie's room and looked in. The little household went to bed with the chickens and rose with the sun.

"Your bed soft?" she inquired, smiling kindly at the little figure with tousled head, whose brown eyes, bright as a squirrel's, peered at his visitor over the patchwork quilt.

At Pyxie's pleased nod, she came in and sat down at his side.

"What kind of a bed did you have at Jenny's house?" inquired Miss Mattie sociably. She had lived alone so long that she found she enjoyed the company and conversation of the little boy. "Did you have a room to yourself as nice as this?"

Pyxie shook his head with a rueful air.

"I didn't have any room," was his answer. "I slept up in the loft. And I didn't have any bed. Only a big heap of rags.

But I didn't mind," he added loyally. "I liked Jenny. Jenny was good to me."

"I know she was. It's right you should stand up for her. She was your friend." Miss Mattie's tone was so understanding that Pyxie was emboldened to say more.

"We used to go to the woods together," said Pyxie, with a smile for past pleasures. "We'd gather berries. Sometimes that was all we had to eat all day. And we would pick flowers, and I'd play in the brook. We'd watch the birds, too, and the fishes, and the little lizards, all brown and green."

"You did?" said Miss Mattie encouragingly. "What else did you do?"

"I didn't catch the fish," went on Pyxie, glad to talk and tell. "I left them there to swim. And I wouldn't touch a bird's nest nor harm an egg for all the world. Jenny said the birds and the fish and all the animals were our friends. It was nice in the woods."

And Pyxie smiled again at the memory of his old, happy-go-lucky, carefree life, with its long hours of idleness and play.

"But it wasn't all nice," said Pyxie, after a moment's thought. "I was hungry lots of times, and cold, and I was afraid of the menfolks, too. I'd a great deal rather be here. I don't want to go back."

And to show that he meant what he said, Pyxie laid a hard little hand confidingly on Miss Mattie's knee.

Miss Mattie took the hand in hers and gave it a friendly shake.

"That's good news," she said heartily. "You want to be here, and I want you to stay. Now, suppose you run down and give James his breakfast. I hear him knocking on the side of his pen."

James was Miss Mattie's pet—a cantankerous, old white gander with hard, staring black eyes and a snapping yellow bill.

This morning, he accepted with a disagreeable hiss the pan of food that Pyxie carried out to him, and his only thanks was a sudden snap at Pyxie's thin brown legs.

The little boy skipped nimbly out of reach and contented himself by making faces, which, to his disappointment, James did not appear to see.

"I want to like you because Miss Mattie does, and you won't let me," said Pyxie reproachfully to the cross old fellow. "But I'm going to be good to you just the same."

And in proof of this fine spirit, he filled James' drinking pan with fresh water from the pump.

A little later, his morning tasks finished, Pyxie seated himself on the back doorstep. Cared for and well fed, he looked very different now from the untidy, neglected boy whom Amanda had brought home from the woods. The blouse he wore was neat and clean. His faded overalls had been washed and so cleverly mended that they answered as well as new. His unruly hair had been brushed until it was flat and glossy, like a bird's wing, while his face fairly glowed from the plentiful use of soap and water, upon which Miss Mattie laid great stress.

He sat there, watching with longing a flight of birds that skimmed by, far overhead.

"If I could just get to the woods," he was thinking, "I know 'twould be nice there today. But I don't believe Miss

Mattie would like it if I went. I'd better stay 'round here. I'm going to start school tomorrow, she said. But I'd rather go to the woods any day than go to school."

And Pyxie looked rather solemn as he thought that this was his last day of freedom.

"I don't want to go to school," Pyxie's thoughts ran on. "Jenny didn't think much of learning. She said reading was bad for the eyes. But Miss Mattie wants me to go, so I s'pose I have to."

Suddenly Pyxie sprang to his feet and uttered a cry.

"James!" exclaimed Pyxie, pointing with a short forefinger. "Miss Mattie, look! James is running away."

Hastily Miss Mattie stepped to the door.

Yes, there was James waddling out of the yard toward the road. In some way he had managed to climb out or creep under his pen. He was making low sounds of satisfaction deep in his throat as he moved along, and every now and then he flapped his wings as if in triumph at his escape.

"Run, Pyxie, run!" exclaimed Miss Mattie wildly, struggling with her spectacles which had caught in her hair. "Drive him back! He will be run over! Run! I'm coming too."

Pyxie sped after the runaway with Miss Mattie close behind.

James was out in the road now, waddling along at a fairly good pace. He rocked from side to side as he went. He did not seem to move swiftly, but it was surprising how far ahead of Pyxie he managed to keep.

It was still more surprising when James broke into a run. It was a rocking, rolling kind of a run. His stout yellow legs twinkled steadily over the ground. It was exciting. Pyxie's face grew red, and he swung his arms and began to shout.

"Pyxie!" called Miss Mattie in a little shriek. "Pyxie! He's headed for Mrs. Barr's house! Drive him in!"

And this Pyxie proceeded to do.

With a dash forward, he caught up with James. And by shouting and whirling his arms, aided by frantic clapping

and breathless calls from Miss Mattie, he succeeded in driving the bewildered James over the grass toward the house.

Mrs. Barr, with Thanny peeping from behind her skirt, appeared in the doorway.

"What's all the commotion?" she demanded. "Well, if it isn't that old gander, James! Where's my clothesline?"

And by the time Miss Mattie had reached the back door and sunk, out of breath, on the steps, James was firmly tied to the apple tree, from whose shade he gazed reproachfully out at his mistress, as if it were all her fault.

But when Miss Mattie, rested and refreshed by drinks of water, was ready to go home, James, in a peaceful and chastened frame of mind, was willing to go, too. In a dignified manner, his head in the air, he walked solemnly along at the end of Mrs. Barr's clothesline and allowed himself, surprisingly enough, to be put back into his pen without one snap or hiss.

"He behaves well," said Miss Mattie proudly. "There is more to James than most people think."

Miss Mattie had a word of praise for Pyxie, too, when he went to bed.

"You are a good boy," said Miss Mattie, with a hand on Pyxie's head, smoothing down his flying locks. "You are my 'home boy,' and tomorrow you will be a 'school boy' too."

Pyxie nodded, with a look up into Miss Mattie's face. He hesitated a moment and then spoke out.

"Amanda asked me if I was a 'Piney boy,'" said Pyxie, "and I told her 'yes.' I was one, then, wasn't I, Miss Mattie?"

"Yes, you were," was Miss Mattie's answer. "But it doesn't matter about the name. It's whether you are a good boy or not."

"Yes, ma'am." Pyxie was deep in his own thoughts.

"I wonder if anybody saw me throw stones at James' pen, to make him mad," he was thinking guiltily. "I don't s'pose Miss Mattie would call me a good boy if she did."

But Miss Mattie was speaking again, and her words were pleasant to hear.

"Now you have been called a 'Piney boy,' a 'home boy,' and a 'school boy,'" said Miss Mattie. "And to my way of thinking, the best name of all is 'home boy.'"

Chapter 4

The First Day at School

Miss Mattie stood on the doorstep and waved goodbye to Amanda and Pyxie as they started off to school.

"Pyxie, you look real nice," called Miss Mattie encouragingly as she surveyed the little figure before her in his neat blue suit, his fresh white blouse, and the gay tie made of one of Amanda's red hair ribbons, but so skillfully done that no one would guess the truth.

Miss Mattie had turned and altered and made over the clothes that a neighbor with boys of her own had given her for Pyxie. She meant her "home boy" to look as well as the other children at school.

"The little fellow is going to have a hard enough time, starting in late at school, and a 'Piney boy' and all," kind

Waved goodbye to Amanda and Pyxie

Miss Mattie had thought as she patiently cut and basted and sewed. "He's going to look right if I can make him so."

Now she gazed with pride at her handiwork and hoped this first day at school would go well with "her boy."

"Amanda, you look after Pyxie," she called again. "It's all new to him, you know. I'll be watching for you, Pyxie, when you come home."

And Miss Mattie waved both hands, as if one were not enough, until the children were out of sight.

The schoolhouse, half a mile away, was a small, unpainted building, one room large, one story high. It stood back from the road among the tall grasses and a lilac bush or two. There were trees in the yard, which made it pleasant and shady. Hens and chickens from a nearby house wandered at will through the grass, and a green pump dripped invitingly not far from the door. There were groups of children chattering around the doorstep, and three little girls came running to meet Amanda.

They all seemed to know one another well, and Pyxie felt awkward and shy and afraid among so many strangers.

"I don't like strangers. Jenny didn't like them either," he thought. And he longed to run away and hide.

But Amanda led him straight forward, and he found himself in the schoolroom, a room well filled with desks and seats and crowded with children sitting and standing and moving about.

"There must be a hundred," thought Pyxie, drawing a long breath.

If Amanda could have read his thoughts, she would have laughed, for there were only twenty-five children in the whole school.

Pyxie followed Amanda to the front of the room where the teacher, Miss Grant, sat at her desk. Pyxie eyed her closely, her pretty brown hair, her pleasant face. Behind her, his wandering eyes spied a big, black stove that promised comfort in winter, and a broom, leaning in home-like fashion against the wall.

"He's a new boy," explained Amanda to the teacher. "I brought him to school. He lives near me. His name is Pyxie," she added as Miss Grant opened a large, black book and took up her pen.

"Pyxie what?" asked Miss Grant, smiling at the newcomer. "Everyone has two names, you know."

Pyxie twisted about in shyness and tried to hide behind Amanda. Amanda herself shook her head.

"I don't know his other name, Miss Grant," said Amanda in a low voice. "He is a 'home boy.' He lives with Miss Mattie Earl."

"Oh," said Miss Grant, laying down her pen. "Then I will leave it just Pyxie until I find out his name. How old are you, Pyxie? What class are you in?"

Pyxie shut his lips tight and turned his back. Amanda answered for him again.

"I think he is eight years old," said Amanda. "And he is not in any class because he has never been to school before."

"Oh," said Miss Grant again, looking over Amanda's shoulder at Pyxie. "Well, Amanda—let him sit at the back of the room behind the little children. Perhaps he can go into their class by and by."

Pyxie was hastily shown to his lonely seat. Amanda thrust a book into his hands. "You can look at the pictures," she whispered and hurried off to her place at the front of the room.

The teacher stood before her desk and struck a little bell. The children rose to their feet. The school day had begun.

Pyxie sat with head bent, his eyes on the floor. Everyone else was standing in silence. They seemed to be waiting for something. Perhaps they were waiting for him.

Pyxie didn't know whether to sit still or to stand up. He tried to rise quietly to his feet, but his shoes scraped noisily over the floor, and his elbow knocked the book off his desk with a thud. The teacher looked straight down the room at him, and, though no child turned to stare, Pyxie knew they were laughing. He slid back into his seat and sank as low as he could out of sight.

Pyxie's heart burned within him. He wished he had never come to school. He was not like the other children, he thought to himself. He didn't know what to do. He didn't even know how to stand up without making a noise.

"What's the matter with my name?" thought Pyxie hotly, remembering the teacher's questions that neither he nor Amanda could answer. "Jenny didn't give me two names. Only one. Why did the teacher say 'just Pyxie' like that?"

This was a problem Pyxie couldn't solve, though he pondered over it for what seemed like a long time. But he made up his mind to one thing.

"If everybody else has two names," thought Pyxie, "I'll have them, too. Maybe Miss Mattie will lend me her name. Earl. Pyxie Earl. That sounds all right."

Emboldened by this thought, Pyxie mustered up the courage to raise his eyes and glance about him.

The small children were seated before him on his side of the room. There were little boys in clean blouses with smooth, well-brushed heads. Pyxie's own wild locks had been brushed till they shone. Miss Mattie had seen to that. The little girls bent over their books until their curls and elf-locks touched the page. Everyone was studying hard. Everyone but Pyxie had something to do.

Across the aisle at the back were grouped the middle-sized boys and girls. This was where Pyxie belonged, but of course he couldn't sit there. Why, he couldn't read even the easiest words, he told himself in dismay. A stout boy, whom the teacher called William, smiled over at Pyxie and made a friendly face. But Pyxie turned his shoulder on him. The boy was laughing at him, he thought.

Up in front sat Amanda among the big boys and girls. She was not as old as they, but she was "advanced." That meant she could do the work they did.

Suddenly, Pyxie hated with all his heart the seat in which he found himself.

"I won't sit on this side with the little children," he thought, his face growing an angry red. "What did the teacher put me here for? I won't stay! I don't care if I can't read and spell."

The door was temptingly near his seat. It stood wide open to the sweet spring air.

"I could slip out just as easy," thought Pyxie to himself, his eyes on the wide, blue morning sky and the trees that seemed to beckon him to come. "I could go to the woods. I like it there. I don't care what Miss Mattie says. I don't care about Amanda either."

Perhaps the teacher saw Pyxie's longing gaze fixed on the open door. At any rate, she came down the room toward him and stood beside his desk.

"I think I won't put you in a class now, Pyxie," she was saying. "I will show you how to make letters so you can learn to write. And Amanda will begin to teach you to read. Then, soon, you can go into a class."

Pyxie was glad of something to do. He worked away at the lesson the teacher set him, with his face screwed up and his tongue sticking out of the corner of his mouth. He was awkward in holding the pencil. He had never held one before. The paper slipped about on the desk. Pyxie's cheeks grew red, and he twined his feet together. He ran his fingers through his hair till it stood out every which way. The task seemed a hard one, but it was better than doing nothing, he thought.

When Amanda came to teach him to read, Pyxie again looked out of the open door and wished he could run away without being seen or caught.

"I don't want a girl to teach me," he thought, a scowl on his face. "I hate girls. I hate everybody. I hate school."

But Amanda was a good teacher, and presently Pyxie began to learn, in spite of himself.

"Anyhow, I can run away at recess," he thought.

But he didn't. For when they were dismissed to eat their luncheon, Amanda stayed close at his side. There didn't seem to be a moment when he could slip away.

The afternoon was no better than the morning except that it didn't last so long. Pyxie felt discouraged as the teacher called upon class after class to recite. He watched the children reading with ease stories that he couldn't understand, spelling words he had never heard before, making figures on the blackboard that held no meaning for him. Even the smallest children in school knew more than he.

"I shan't come again," Pyxie promised himself. "I don't know anything. I don't belong here."

But at the very end of the day, Pyxie changed his mind. He heard someone talking about him—a boy named Norman, who whispered to his neighbor, but so loud that Pyxie heard. They were filing out of the room. Amanda was already on the doorstep, Pyxie farther back in the line.

"That boy doesn't know anything," whispered Norman with a nod toward Pyxie. "He isn't even in a class. He can't learn. That's what's the matter with him."

At these words Pyxie's back stiffened. His face grew hot.

"I'll never come here again!" he muttered. "Never!"

Why should he come to a place where he was so despised and so unhappy?

Then a thought struck him, and he almost stood still on his way toward the door.

"If I don't come to school, I can't learn," he thought. "And I want to learn. I want to show them all."

Pyxie straightened up and held his head high.

"I will come to school. I'll have to come. I can learn as fast as anybody else. I know I can. And I will."

Pyxie's heart was full of this new ambition when he joined Amanda in the yard. But he could not tell her what he had overheard nor of his thoughts and plans.

He stopped long enough to sit down by the roadside and take off his stiff, heavy shoes. He cooled and stretched his hot toes in the long, soft grass. Then he and Amanda, glad of their liberty, ran toward home.

And all the way, Pyxie was thinking, "I can learn. I know I can learn. Someday I will be in a class like the rest, and then I'll show what I can do."

Miss Mattie was watching for them as she had promised. All day her thoughts had been with Pyxie, hoping he would do well in school.

Now she called from the doorway. "How did you like it? How did school go?"

"All right. It was first-rate," answered Pyxie, carelessly swinging his luncheon-pail.

He wasn't ready yet to tell what he really thought and felt.

"He did well," supplied Amanda loyally. "I'm teaching him to read. He has learned three words already. And the teacher is showing him how to write."

"I knew it." Miss Mattie turned and smiled upon Pyxie with pride. "You will have to work hard to catch up with the rest, but that won't take you long, once you get a start."

Pyxie didn't answer. He couldn't say what was in his mind until Amanda had gone home. He even waited until he and Miss Mattie were alone on the steps, after supper, in the dark.

"Miss Mattie," began Pyxie, moving a little closer to his friend in the dusk, "I didn't have two names in school today. I only had one. Everybody else has two names but me."

"Why, Pyxie—" began Miss Mattie.

But Pyxie, full of his own thoughts, went on, "I thought maybe you wouldn't mind lending me your name, Miss Mattie. I'd like to have the teacher put down Pyxie Earl in the book, not just Pyxie, like it is now."

Miss Mattie answered quickly, "I never thought about your name, Pyxie," she said. "Yes, you take mine. You tell the teacher to put you down as Pyxie Earl."

"There was a boy today in school; he said I couldn't learn," said Pyxie. "But I can learn. I am going to work hard and show them all. I'm going to show that I can do as well as all the rest."

Miss Mattie caught Pyxie's hand and gave it a little squeeze.

"Of course you can do as well," said Miss Mattie warmly. "I wouldn't be surprised if you did better. Why, it wouldn't surprise me if you did the best of all."

"Maybe I will," said Pyxie.

Chapter 5

The Green Van

"Something nice is going to happen today, Pyxie."

"What, Amanda? What's going to happen?"

Pyxie and Amanda were on their way to school. It was a gay spring morning: blue sky, bright sunshine, flowers blooming in the meadows and beside the road.

Pyxie trudged faithfully along at Amanda's side. Every day had found him in his place at school. He still meant to prove that he could learn. He still meant to show his little world at school that he could do as well as they.

To be sure, he had set himself a long, slow task. It was so easy to forget, and the pencil wouldn't do what he wanted, and as for numbers, Pyxie would gladly have seen them all thrown into the sea.

But Miss Mattie encouraged him at home. "Don't you give up, Pyxie," she said. "You are going to come out ahead. Wait and see."

And at school Miss Grant told him, more than once, that he did learn, little by little, day by day.

Now, seeing that Amanda's good news was ready to tumble off the tip of her tongue, he asked again, eagerly, "What is going to happen, Amanda? Tell me, do."

"Miss Bird is coming today to bring us different books," answered Amanda, smiling at the very thought. "I love it the day she comes. I like the books, and I like her, too. She tells us stories, and she makes us all laugh."

And Amanda gave a lively skip and whirl in the grass that set the daisies to nodding and made the Queen Anne's lace sway to and fro.

At this news, so pleasing to Amanda, Pyxie's face lost its smile.

This was a day that he had dreaded ever since he had first gone to school and heard of Miss Bird, the Book Lady, who would come driving in her little library van, bringing books to everyone.

"Everybody in school knows I can't read," thought Pyxie, his steps growing slower and slower as school drew more near. "But the Book Lady doesn't know it. She will want to give me a book, and I won't know what to say."

Pyxie stood still in the road. He let Amanda walk on ahead.

"She will ask me questions," he was thinking. "She will ask me what class I am in and what books I have read.

When she finds out that I can't read, maybe she'll laugh. Then everybody else will laugh at me, too. I won't go. I won't go to school today."

And Pyxie, after one glance at Amanda, stepping serenely along the road, made up his mind that he would run away.

It was easy to climb the roadside fence. It was pleasant running through the meadow grass with the wind whistling past his ears. He waved a carefree hand to Amanda staring in amazement from the roadside. A saucy smile over his shoulder was the only answer he made to her shrill calls.

Through the meadow, over another fence, and he was in the woods, the familiar, friendly woods, where there were no strangers, nor questions, nor tasks.

Shouting and running wildly through the dry leaves, lying on the brown carpet of pine needles just to get his breath, playing in the noisy brook, Pyxie thought how wise he had been to run away from school. How simple a way out, too! Why had he ever troubled himself about Miss Bird and her books?

It was not quite so simple to explain his running away to

Miss Mattie and Miss Grant, as Pyxie learned a little later on. He listened in silence to what they had to say. But all the while he was telling himself, over and over, "Anyway, I didn't have to see the Book Lady, and she didn't see me."

Now, not long after, he and Amanda were again on their way to school. The little girl, made wary by his escapade, kept a sharp eye upon every step he took.

"Come on, Pyxie. I'm afraid we'll be late."

"No, we won't, Amanda. There's lots of time. See those two airships? Don't they look like big, silver fish?"

And Pyxie, his head tilted back, leisurely watched the two great dirigibles, from the nearby Naval Air Station, move steadily along, glittering brightly in the morning sun.

"Do you want to be late? Don't you like school?" Amanda's gaze was fixed on Pyxie. She refused to look up at the familiar sight overhead. "You have only missed two days so far, once with the toothache and once when you ran away."

"Yes, I like school," answered Pyxie slowly, his eyes still on the sky. "But I don't like it as well as I might."

"Why not? What do you mean?" Amanda spoke sharply. She felt this was ungrateful in a pupil she had tried so hard to teach. "You know you are learning fast. You can read 'most half the First Reader, and Miss Grant said she might put you in a class before long."

"Did she say that?" Pyxie brightened. "Well, I'll tell you, Amanda. This is the way I feel. I don't like what you learn in school. I don't like it as well as the woods."

"Whatever do you mean?" asked Amanda again, slowly, standing still by the roadside, quite forgetting the school clock. "What don't you like in school?"

"Everything," replied Pyxie largely. "Everything you learn. You have to say the same things over and over, and you read the same stories till I'm tired of hearing them. I don't care about the stories in my reader. I don't want to read. And I don't want to learn how to figure and write and spell."

"But you have to know," said Amanda, somewhat bewildered by these new ideas. "Suppose you want to farm, or keep a store, or run a cranberry bog. You would have to know how to figure and read and spell."

"But I'm never going to keep a store or do any of those things," said Pyxie decidedly. "I'm going to live in the woods. I like it there best. And you like it, too, Amanda, the time you and Thanny and me took our lunch and stayed all day. You know you did."

"Of course I liked it," admitted Amanda frankly. "But that doesn't mean you shouldn't go to school."

"Wasn't it fun to watch the little fishes in the brook? And remember all the birds and the different kinds of nests they build? And the frogs' eggs we brought home? Mine are turning into tadpoles in a bucket out on the back porch. There's more sense in that, Amanda, than saying over and over that two times two are four."

"You have to know it all," decided Amanda, after a little thought. "It is good to know about the woods. But

"Wasn't it fun to watch the little fishes in the brook?"

you have to know how to read and write and figure, too. Everybody does, everybody that knows anything at all. Anyway, we'll have to run now, or we will be late. Come on."

Amanda had spoken truly when she said that Pyxie was learning fast. Already he could read several stories in his reader. He knew a few numbers, too. And Miss Mattie had brought out his favorite jam for supper the day he proudly carried home his name—PYXIE EARL—written in large, uneven letters that roamed across the paper straight downhill.

This morning from his seat near the door, Pyxie looked out over the crowded schoolroom, humming with low voices. There sat Amanda up in front, her crimson hair ribbon standing above her smooth dark head. The little children buzzed busily together over their books. Plump William grinned cheerfully from across the aisle at Pyxie, who responded with a fleeting little smile and then bent over his desk.

For Pyxie was still shy. It was hard for him to mingle with the other children in friendly give and take.

"I feel like they are strangers, all but Amanda," Pyxie explained to himself.

On the other hand, the children did not understand Pyxie, quiet and bashful and aloof.

"He won't play with us," complained the children when he slipped away from their chatter and their games. "He is a 'fraid-cat. He's afraid to play."

And they taunted him with "'fraid-cat" and "scary" when the valiant Amanda was not near.

As he sat there, Pyxie was thinking of all this, his mind wandering from his task.

"But I like Amanda," thought Pyxie, "and I like Miss Grant. She helps me and teaches me a lot when she has time."

Pyxie was in an idle mood that morning. Indeed, there was a spirit of expectancy hovering over the whole school.

What did it mean? Never before had so many children required drinks of water at the pump. The slightest sound made all eyes turn toward the open door. And why did everyone who passed a window stop to peer out?

Soon, in a whisper, a rumor went round and round the room.

"Miss Bird is coming. The Book Lady is coming today."

This was news to Pyxie. Why hadn't Amanda told him? Oh, if only he dared to run away again!

"Maybe she won't see me," he thought hopefully. "Maybe she will walk right past my desk."

It was in the early afternoon that a little girl stepped demurely out to the pump for her third drink of water. A second later she came flying back into the room. She brought excitement with her. Forgotten for the moment were all Miss Grant's orders and rules. Every head was turned, and some of the children half rose from their seats.

"She's come! She's come!" shrieked the little girl from the doorway. "The Book Lady has come! And the book wagon, too! They are almost here. She's come!"

Down went pencils and papers and books. Every child in the room twisted around in his seat toward the door. Miss Grant herself left her desk and her work and walked down the aisle.

There was the roll of wheels coming nearer. And here was the van, in the schoolyard, stopping before the very door. It was a small, trim van, painted a dark and glossy green and neatly lettered in gold.

Pyxie drew a long breath. He was caught. A moment more and the Book Lady herself would be in the room.

Chapter 6

The Book Lady

In the doorway stood the Book Lady. Pyxie stared at her with all his might.

He saw a lady with gay blue eyes and a wide smile and hair that was yellow, yellow as the sun. The hair curled out from under her hat, and it was so bright that it seemed as if it had caught the sunshine and brought it into the room.

The Book Lady stood in the doorway without saying a word and smiled. Her eyes held a twinkle, and her mouth took on a funny little quirk. The smile was so catching that it made everyone else smile, too, even Pyxie.

So this was the Book Lady! This was the person from whom he had run away!

In the doorway stood the Book Lady.

"She doesn't look as if she would ask questions or make fun of anybody," thought Pyxie, his eyes still fixed on her face.

The Book Lady, after a word with Miss Grant, stepped into the room.

"Well, children," she said—and when the Book Lady spoke, she made them all feel as if she were glad to be there and to see them again— "Well, children, have you read all the books I brought you? And do you want more?"

It seemed as if the school were only waiting for this question. The very next second every tongue was loosed.

"Miss Bird, I want another book about forest animals."

"Miss Bird, my mother read me my book. It was about a dog and a cat that ran away. I liked it."

"I want another book about the twins that lived somewhere else but here. I just had one about the twins that lived in Japan."

"And Toby Tyler ran away with the circus, and he had a monkey named Mr. Stubbs."

Everyone talked at once, and the Book Lady seemed to like it. She stood there and listened and smiled. The children not only told what they had read, they told what they wanted to read next.

Amanda asked for "that book, you know, Miss Bird, about a girl named Rebecca who had a parasol and rode in the stagecoach. You know the one I mean."

Plump William, who secretly longed to be a cowboy and who spent hours trying to lasso the pump at home, thought he would like something about Buffalo Bill.

"Yes, yes, I have books for everyone. The van is full," promised Miss Bird. "Somebody must help me carry out the books that have been read. You, Norman and William, you help me today. And those who want another book may come out to the van and choose."

In little groups, the children trooped out and, shortly after, came back, each with a book into which they peeped with delighted exclamations and smiles.

Only Pyxie sat still. It was all very well for the Book Lady to bring to the children books that they wanted to read. It was well enough, too, to take the books home, if they liked. But Pyxie didn't want a book. He didn't want to read. He didn't like books. "A cat, a mouse, and a hen lived in a house." That was what his reader said. Books were dull.

"Now has everyone the book he wants?" The Book Lady was back in the schoolroom and was walking around among the desks with a word for every child. "Amanda, you have *Rebecca of Sunnybrook Farm*? And, Norman, you took *Treasure Island*? Yes, John, *Toby Tyler* is a good story. Your friend liked it and you will, too. Of course I've read about So-Fat and Mew-Mew, little Ann. Weren't you glad when they reached home again?"

Miss Bird was walking toward Pyxie. She stopped beside his desk.

"You didn't get a book," said Miss Bird in her friendly voice. "You are a new boy, aren't you? I haven't seen you before."

Pyxie couldn't answer. He stared in front of him in silence.

But Amanda, hovering near, with her book clasped in her arms, came to the rescue.

"He is new, Miss Bird," volunteered Amanda. "He is my friend, and his name is Pyxie. He can't read very well yet. That's why he doesn't want a book, I guess."

"What do you think he would like?" asked Miss Bird of Amanda. She didn't seem to mind at all that Pyxie had turned his back. "What does he like to do himself?"

"He likes the woods," said Amanda quickly. "He knows lots of the birds and where they build their nests. And the fishes, too, he likes. And he knows just when the different flowers come."

"I like birds, too, Pyxie." The Book Lady looked pleased. "Come out to the van with Amanda and me. I have the very book for you there."

In the yard, Miss Bird swung open the double doors at the back of the van, and Pyxie, on tip-toe, peering in, saw shelves tightly packed with books, row on row.

There were large books and small books, books thin and thick, of every color and hue. The sight meant little or nothing to Pyxie. But Amanda was more wise.

The little girl knew what she and the other children had found among these books—pleasure, and beauty, and information, as well. Here were happy hours, spent, it might be, in a world where the good and the noble and the lovely triumphed over wrong and selfishness in a most satisfactory way. Here, too, were to be found new and lasting friends. They might be great heroes of history or of legend, like gallant Drake, or wise and patient Lincoln, or King Arthur and his Round Table. Perhaps they were children like themselves, perhaps living in other lands, with other customs and ways. There were books to suit every taste. There were tales of stirring adventure, of sports at school, animal stories, and books that told of life in the woods and fields nearby.

It was a book of this kind that Miss Bird now offered to Pyxie.

"Hop up on the step with me," invited Miss Bird. "Now go inside and pull out that blue book with a black bird on the back. Now you look at that book, Pyxie, and see if you wouldn't like to take it home."

Pyxie, Amanda peering over his shoulder, opened the book with clumsy little hands.

There was very little reading in this book. But on every page was a bird, the colored picture of a bird and her nest and eggs.

Pyxie, with a look of delight, at once recognized the bird to which he had opened. It was like meeting an old friend.

"That's a woodpecker!" exclaimed Pyxie. "It looks just like him, too, all black and white and red. There's the hole he has for a nest. What's this over here? A robin! I knew it. There is his name underneath. R-o-b-i-n." And Pyxie, to Amanda's pride, slowly spelled out the word. "Robin. That spells robin. My, this is a fine book!"

His face aglow, he smiled up at Miss Bird, who, seemingly as pleased as he, smiled back.

"You take it home, Pyxie," said Miss Bird, shutting the van doors with a slam. "When you have finished with it, I will give you another that you will like just as well. Now I must go back and say goodbye to the children and hurry along."

In the schoolroom, the children were watching for Miss Bird's return.

"Don't go!" they clamored. "Don't go yet! Tell us a story. Tell us two, Miss Bird."

The Book Lady looked at her watch.

"Just one story today," she said briskly, "for I have another school to visit, and there are people waiting for books all along the road. Somebody wants a cookbook, a man with a broken leg wants a funny book, and somebody wants to know what to do when his hens have the gapes. But I have time for just one story."

It was a funny story, about all the scrapes a boy fell into, and how his animal friends helped him out.

Pyxie liked the story. It made him laugh. Everyone was laughing, even Miss Grant. And from the look on her face and the light in her eye, you could tell that Miss Bird liked the story, too.

Pyxie did not take his eyes from Miss Bird's face. Why, she wasn't at all as he had thought she would be. She hadn't asked him a single question. She knew what you would like to read without making you tell.

Amid a great waving of hands and calling of goodbyes, the little van rolled out of the yard. Pyxie watched it through the open door until it was out of sight.

"There, now, Pyxie, you have a book, too." Amanda stopped at his desk before she went to her seat, and the school settled down again to work. "You said this morning that you didn't like books. I guess you didn't mean it, after all."

"I like this one," said Pyxie, holding his blue book fast and wishing he could run home and show it to Miss Mattie that very moment. "It's a real book. It's about something. It makes sense. And I guess Miss Mattie is going to like it, too."

Chapter 7

Miss Grant Asks a Question

Pyxie was right. Miss Mattie did like his bird book. They spent evening after evening looking at the pictures and spelling out the names of the birds. Miss Mattie read to him, too, the little story about each bird, how he looked, and where he lived and built his nest.

After an early supper, they would settle themselves on the narrow front porch, where Miss Mattie's rocking chair, with its turkey-red cushions, swayed to and fro, and Pyxie's little bench waited for its owner to come. But often they sat on the step together, sharing the book, side by side.

They looked contented and happy sitting there, wiry little Miss Mattie, her neat gray head bent over the page, and Pyxie, round-eyed, pressing close to her knee, his finger triumphantly pointing out a familiar word.

Looking at the pictures and spelling out the names of the birds

Behind them, the windows of the little white house flamed rosy-red in the sunset glow. Sweet odors floated up to them from the old-fashioned garden flowers that thickly bordered the path. There were spicy pinks, cloudy purple heliotrope, mignonette, foxglove, and nodding Canterbury bells. The pungent smell of lemon verbena and the cool scent of mint mingled pleasantly at the fall of dew.

It was the happiest hour of the day, Pyxie thought. As for Miss Mattie, she enjoyed the reading quite as well as did the little boy.

"Why don't you ask for another book?" she suggested when the bird book had been read from cover to cover. "Let's try something else."

Miss Bird seemed to know just what Pyxie wanted. The story of a little rabbit followed the bird book, and the funny tale of a big black bear came after that.

Miss Mattie read the stories over and over until Pyxie almost could say them by heart. He pored over the pictures and picked out all the words he knew. He learned some new ones, too.

Then one evening, encouraged by Miss Mattie, Pyxie took his turn at reading aloud, which he did surprisingly well, with help over only the longest, hardest words.

"I can truly read now, can't I?" said Pyxie, as, flushed with triumph, he brought the little story safely to an end. He and Miss Mattie smiled happily at one another. It would be hard to say which one felt more proud. "This isn't like reading in my reader. This is a real, true book."

And Pyxie hugged the big red book close as if it were a friend.

"I like books better now," he confided shyly to Amanda, who was so pleased at this news that she couldn't resist calling it out to Miss Bird the very next time she came.

"Pyxie likes books now," announced Amanda, proud of her pupil. "He doesn't hate reading anymore. And he likes you, too. He keeps asking how many more days before you are going to come."

Pyxie's face was scarlet. He slid down in his seat as far as he could go. How could Amanda call out that way about him before the whole school?

But Miss Bird was laughing so gaily and Amanda was looking so pleased that Pyxie couldn't be as angry as he wished. He muttered under his breath and made faces. But Miss Bird understood, for when she passed his seat she gave his arm the friendliest kind of a shake.

Before long, Pyxie had left picture books behind him. More and more often, too, he was able to take his turn at reading aloud.

One day, he came running home from school waving a book in the air.

"It's about a man named Boone, Daniel Boone!" he called from the road in a shout.

He stumbled hastily up the steps and thrust the little bright green volume into Miss Mattie's hands. "He liked the woods same as me. And he fought the Indians. Can't we have supper early so we can have a long time to read?"

Many were the happy hours Pyxie and Miss Mattie spent reading to one another, turn by turn, the story, told in simple language, of this famous woodsman, hunter, and pioneer.

"I wish I'd lived then," said Pyxie, eyeing with longing the picture of the gallant figure in his hunting suit and coonskin cap with his long gun in his hand and his dog at his knee.

"It is just as exciting today, and more so," said Miss Mattie.

And her words were proved true when Pyxie brought home a simple story of Lindbergh, flying alone over the ocean, and of Byrd, who braved the darkness and the peril and the cold of the farthest southern seas.

"I don't know which one I like the best," said Pyxie when the last story was ended and the book was regretfully closed. "I don't know which one I wish I could be."

"Can't you like them all?" inquired Miss Mattie. "They are all fine, brave men."

"Seems as if they weren't afraid of anything," mused Pyxie, remembering how he was called "'fraid-cat" at school. "They weren't afraid of people nor of being cold nor hungry nor being hurt. I wonder if they were ever afraid of anything at all."

And Pyxie devoted a few moments to wishing he had been born as brave as they and then to making up his mind to be like them, if he could.

"The reason they are brave is because they are never thinking of themselves," said Miss Mattie wisely. "They are thinking of other people and other things. That is why they are not afraid."

"Yes, ma'am," answered Pyxie thoughtfully. "I guess that's true."

May had gone, and June with its sunshine and its roses was here. In a few weeks' time, school would close for the long summer holiday.

It was at the end of a warm, sleepy day when the bees hummed in and out of the windows, and everyone was keeping close watch on the school clock, that Miss Grant stood before her desk and asked a question that made every scholar sit up straight in his seat.

"Before school closes for the summer," said Miss Grant, scanning the children row by row and face by face, "wouldn't you like to give Miss Bird a surprise right here in school?"

"Yes! Yes!" came from all parts of the room, even from Pyxie's corner, and quite a loud shout from him, at that.

"Shall we talk about it, then," said Miss Grant, "and plan what we should like to do?"

For the next few moments, the air was filled with the sound of many voices. Everyone had something to say, something to suggest. Now and then the room grew quiet while Miss Grant talked earnestly, with twenty-five pairs of round eyes fixed unwinking on her face. Then hands shot up here and there, and little voices piped out what they thought the best and pleasantest thing to do.

"It's going to be fun," said Amanda, in high satisfaction, when they had settled on a plan. "Won't Miss Bird laugh? I am glad it's a secret, too. We mustn't tell."

And chattering busily, the twenty-five children filed out of school to run home with this unusual and delightful secret burning on their tongues.

Every house that held a school child was thrown into confusion that afternoon.

"Miss Mattie! Miss Mattie! Where are you?" Pyxie dashed into the kitchen, scattering books and papers and pencils as he ran. "It's a surprise and a secret, but I can tell you. Miss Grant said so. Where are you? I want to tell!"

"Good gracious me!" Miss Mattie hurried down from upstairs. "What's happened? Look at your face, red as fire. Sit down and cool off."

And Miss Mattie tried to press Pyxie into a chair, from which he bounced up immediately like a rubber ball.

"It's a surprise for Miss Bird," explained Pyxie, hastily wiping his hot face with his sleeve. "We are all going to dress up and be somebody else. Who shall I be? It's a secret! You mustn't tell!"

At this news, Miss Mattie was as pleased and almost as excited as Pyxie himself. She sank into the big kitchen rocker and began a steady swaying back and forth.

"You stand still, Pyxie Earl," she commanded, catching the little boy by the sleeve. "Tell me all about it from A to Z."

This Pyxie proceeded to do, with many interruptions from Miss Mattie, and the conversation lasted without pause until it was time to put the kettle on for tea.

For the next two weeks, the air of the entire neighborhood was filled with secrets. Groups of children whispered and laughed on their way to and from school. The schoolyard hummed with voices, and at odd moments there was great buzzing in the classroom itself. Miss Grant spent every spare minute talking and planning with this one and that, while sometimes the whole school joined in to give its opinion and help.

Amanda and Pyxie had so much to say to one another that their tongues wagged merrily whenever they met. There was always something to tell and talk over.

"My mother is going over to your house today," confided Amanda, lowering her voice and glancing over her shoulder, though there was no one near them on the lonely country road. "Miss Mattie is going to help her with my dress."

"Miss Mattie has borrowed a cap for me," responded Pyxie with pride. "It looks just like the picture. And it isn't much too big."

"Father will be down at the schoolhouse tonight," reported Amanda. "Miss Grant and some of the mothers will be there, too. Father is going to fix the curtain so it will pull apart on a cord."

"Did you know," asked Pyxie, looking as happy as it is possible for a little boy to look—"did you know that maybe Miss Mattie is going to buy me a gun—maybe?"

"No, is she?" Amanda gave an excited little laugh and skip. "Isn't it fun? Now Thanny wants to be in the surprise, too. Mother is going to see if she can't work him in."

There was great excitement in school the day the invitation to Miss Bird was written and sent. And still more excitement when her answer came.

"She's coming! She's coming!" the word went around. "She thinks it is a regular entertainment. She doesn't guess a thing."

"Wouldn't it be dreadful if somebody met Miss Bird and told?" suggested William, losing his usual cheerful look, for the moment, at the very idea.

"We won't tell," hastily promised the little children, alarmed by the looks of suspicion that were at once cast in their direction. "We only tell our mothers. Miss Grant said we might."

"Of course we won't tell," chorused the other children, solemnly crossing their fingers and laying their hands on their hearts.

"There isn't one of us mean enough to tell Miss Bird," said Amanda, with a confidence which Miss Grant shared. "I guess we all know how to keep a secret. But I do wish the day would hurry. Sometimes I think it is never going to be here."

Chapter 8

A Surprise for Miss Bird

It was the day of the surprise. In spite of Amanda's feelings and forebodings, it had come at last.

The schoolroom looked tidy and unfamiliar and gay with flowers on every windowsill and not a book nor pencil in sight.

A great brown curtain, borrowed from the church, hid from view the stage built by Mr. Barr at the front of the room. It supplied a delightful air of mystery and suggested all sorts of exciting and unusual sights soon to be revealed.

In the early afternoon, the mothers, dressed in their best, began to gather. They fitted themselves with much talk and laughter into the children's seats. From behind the curtain came whispering and laughing, with now and then the glimpse of a pair of feet or a round, curious, peering eye.

Miss Mattie and Mrs. Barr, with Thanny, starched and shining, came in together. The little boy was hastily smuggled behind the scenes, while Mrs. Barr stationed herself beside the curtain. She was to pull it open and shut.

Then Miss Bird came. Everyone could hear the little green van roll into the yard. The mothers smiled at one another and settled themselves as comfortably as they could in their small seats. They knew the surprise that was to come. Behind the curtain there was a ripple of excitement that threatened to overflow into the room.

Miss Bird, gay in a pretty blue dress that matched her eyes, was directed to the front seat that had been saved for her. A bunch of flowers had been tied upon the arm of the chair to show that it was meant for an honored guest. Miss Bird seemed to know everyone in the room. She nodded and smiled about her and then sat back with an expectant air.

It was time to begin.

Miss Grant stepped out before the curtain. In her best company manner, she made a little speech of welcome to the guests. She vanished, and there was a pause.

Then slowly, with jerks and twitches, the curtains moved apart and disclosed a little girl sitting alone on the stage.

The little girl wore a most familiar look. Her long, red hair was parted into two thick braids that hung over her shoulders. She was dressed in an old-fashioned, long-sleeved frock, well covered by a neat white pinafore. She wore long, white stockings, and on her feet were little black boots, laced up to her ankles. She was Anne Shirley, happy in her new-found home, Green Gables, which was delightfully prepared for a party.

Upon a knock at Anne's door, other costumed children appeared on stage in a most amusing scene. Such distinguished guests had never before set foot in the little schoolroom.

Topsy, straight out of *Uncle Tom's Cabin*, came in with a lively skip and a bound, her woolly pigtails flying.

Dashing Buffalo Bill appeared, wearing a splendid cowboy suit and whirling his lasso.

Hans Brinker, in his clumsy wooden shoes appeared on stage. Robin Hood and his Merry Men, with a great brandishing of bows and arrows, marched boldly to their places along the wall.

The fearless, manly spirit of this group was in great contrast to the behavior of a timid little Indian maiden named Chi-Wee, who had to be supported, not to say pulled, by the hand of Katrinka of Russia before she could be persuaded to show herself to the crowded room.

Here was Toby, round-faced and rosy, carrying upon his shoulder a borrowed stuffed monkey, which was almost too lifelike for the peace of mind of timid little Chi-Wee.

In tripped Rebecca of Sunnybrook Farm, an old-fashioned little girl in a glossy, buff calico dress, wearing a little straw bonnet and actually carrying a gay pink parasol in her hand. Anne and Rebecca smiled at one another, and their looks plainly said, "We would be good friends if only we knew one another."

Daniel Boone, the famous woodsman, stepped from behind the screen, bold as a lion, no doubt, but looking, at sight of so many people, as frightened as if he were being dragged to an Indian stake. He was clad in a brown muslin hunting costume, while on his head rested a real coonskin cap, with striped bushy tail hanging down behind. In his arms he held a gun, a new and shining gun.

Daniel Boone made a stiff bow to his hostess and then hastily hid himself in the row behind the flowing cape of Red Riding Hood, who had followed on his heels. He pushed back his cap which, to his embarrassment, at the most unexpected moments fell forward over his face. Then, over Red Riding Hood's shoulder, his eyes searched the room for Miss Mattie and sent her a quick and happy glance. One hand lovingly fingered the trigger of his gun, while the other stole up now and then to pat the splendid furry tail of his cap.

The Eskimo Twins, in spite of the June day, each presented Anne with a large and glittering snowball.

Now the last guest, and also the smallest, impatient for his turn to come, could be seen peeping out from behind the screen. He was a plump little George Washington, in knee breeches and snowy cotton wig, with a bunch of ripe cherries clutched in his hand. He made a dramatic entry by tripping over his hatchet and falling upon his knees.

After one startled cry of "'Manda!" George Washington was gently set upon his feet and given in charge of Rebecca of Sunnybrook Farm, who wisely fed him the cherries he still carried and thus restored him to a proper calm.

All the guests having been welcomed, the gaiety now began. There was to be music, plenty of it, and the orchestra, composed of Robin Hood and his Merry Men, fetched their instruments from behind the screen and stationed themselves at the side of the stage.

There is nothing more gay and stirring than the sound of the fife and drum, and all over the room, feet began to tap when the band broke forth into a merry tune. It is true that the number of their selections was limited. "Dixie" and "Yankee Doodle" were the only tunes they were able to play, with the exception of "Onward, Christian Soldiers," in a pinch. But of course no one was rude enough to notice this lack of variety. The band skillfully changed the time of the music to fit the need. And the dancers were most accommodating, overlooking any little lapse or flaw.

As was natural and proper, the children broke out in a spirited polka. They stepped aside for Katrinka, who, in her bright Russian costume, vigorously whirled and stamped and twirled as blithely as she might once have danced before the Czar himself.

Not willing to have his country outdone, Hans Brinker and his wooden shoes upheld the honor of Holland in a dance which charmed Thanny, in particular, both by its noisy thumping and the uncertainty as to whether the wooden shoes would stay on to the end.

Daniel Boone made a stiff bow to his hostess.

Now a happy medley, Red Riding Hood and Chi-Wee danced on nimble toes until they were out of breath. And they were followed by Santa Claus, who favored them with a lively Highland Fling, which, of course, he must have seen at many a Christmas party as he journeyed through Scotland's low-hung gray skies on Christmas Eve.

Last of all came Topsy in a plantation jig, her eyes sparkling and her pigtails flying—a tapping, leaping, heel-and-toe jig that lasted until the band, red in the face and breathless, dropped their fifes and drumsticks and, for the moment, could play no more.

But they recovered in time to make music for the tripping, dancing rings, one within another, which took in everyone, from George Washington, whose plump legs, for whole moments at a time, did not touch the floor, up to tall Buffalo Bill, whose fancy steps and capers were the admiration of the entire room.

Then the rings parted and changed. To the martial strains of "Yankee Doodle," two by two, everyone fell in line for the Grand March, and soon all were moving briskly around the stage and down into the room.

They made a fine showing.

Round and round the room they all went, up and down the aisles and back again. Their feet kept time to the gay strains of the old war song and "Yankee Doodle," with a bit of "Onward, Christian Soldiers," thrown in just to vary the tune.

The mothers were laughing and bending forward in their seats. Miss Mattie's face was filled with pride as her eyes followed Pyxie around the room. Miss Grant looked flushed and happy. Mr. Barr and a few other fathers leaned in at the open window and laughed at the sight.

But Miss Bird! The Book Lady! What did she think of this surprise?

You had only to look at her to know how pleased and happy she felt. She smiled straight into the face of every child who passed her chair. And when, after five times around the room, Robin Hood and his Merry Men were forced to mop their brows and gasp for breath, it was Miss Bird who led the applause and clapped the loudest, too.

Then, when at last the room had grown quiet, Miss Bird made a little speech.

She told what a surprise this entertainment had been to her—one of the biggest surprises in all her life—and how very happy she felt to be there among so many friends, friends in books and friends out of them as well.

"And now," said Miss Bird, as she looked about the crowded room, "I have something pleasant to say to you. Last summer, when school closed, no one out here had any books to read until school opened again in the fall. This year, all summer, I will bring books to those who want them—to grown people and to children, too."

This was good news, indeed! Everyone began to talk at once, to tell what he or she wanted to read.

But in the excitement and confusion, Miss Bird felt a touch on her hand. She looked down to see the little hunter Daniel Boone, his coonskin cap pushed back on his head and his glittering gun held tight in his hands.

He was looking up with bright and happy eyes.

"We want books, Miss Bird," said Pyxie. Forgotten was his shyness in what he had to say. "We both want books, Miss Mattie and me. And, Miss Bird, say, did you see my gun?"

Chapter 9

A Day's Ride

"Pyxie, don't I hear wheels a-coming?"

"Yes, ma'am, I hear them, too. But I don't see the book wagon and Miss Bird yet. The road is empty, both ways."

"Well, look sharp now. We don't want to let her get by without stopping here."

"No, ma'am. We don't."

And Pyxie, like Sister Anne on the tower, peered from under his hand along the white, sandy road.

It was vacation time and hot summer weather. True to her promise, Miss Bird, every so often, came driving by in the little green County Library van filled with treasures to suit the most varied tastes. She was eagerly watched for and welcomed by many in this scattered and lonely neighborhood. It seemed nowadays as if in almost every household someone was reading a library book. Warm days and long, dull evenings, the busyness of farm and house work, were forgotten in stories that carried their readers to all corners of the earth and gave them an interest and a part in fresh scenes and thrilling adventures.

"Miss Mattie! She's coming! Here she is!"

Pyxie's shrill call brought Miss Mattie out into the front yard while the little boy darted into the road and stood there with outstretched arms, barring the way.

The green van, bowling smoothly and swiftly along, came to a stop just comfortably short of Pyxie's bare toes. Miss Bird, her blue eyes crinkled with laughter at this bold gesture, stepped down from the car and joined Miss Mattie in the yard.

"Miss Bird," began Miss Mattie at once, brandishing a plump, brown volume as she spoke, "here is *Old Curiosity Shop* back again, and I never read a better book. I laughed, and I cried. Some of it I read out loud to Pyxie, and I can tell you we both got pretty well worked up over the death of little Nell. Now I want another one just as good."

Miss Bird led the way to the van and swung back the doors. She opened the side flaps, too, behind which were cunningly hidden shelves filled with books. Pyxie was walking around the car, surveying it with an air of ownership. He couldn't help feeling that Miss Bird was his special friend. If it hadn't been for him, Miss Mattie might never have known her at all.

"I want a thick book because now I read so fast," said Pyxie, hopping up on the step with the ease of practice and seating himself on a little stool inside. "Come right in, Miss Mattie. Don't you be afraid. Miss Bird won't mind. Come in and look 'round."

At this cordial invitation, Miss Mattie and Miss Bird exchanged smiles which Pyxie, peering along the shelves, did not see.

"I want a book about elephants and lions and tigers," he was saying. "We are going to the circus someday, Amanda and Thanny and me. Mr. Barr said so. I want to know how the men catch the animals and bring them home to the circus here."

When the books had been chosen and the van doors shut, Miss Bird asked a question.

"Would anyone like to go driving today?" she said with her droll little smile. "I brought lunch enough for two."

"Me?" Pyxie's face was bright.

Miss Mattie looked pleased, too.

"He can go," she said promptly. "He has been a real good boy all week. Run wash your face and hands, Pyxie. And I'll tie up a little pie, just big enough for you two."

Pyxie, scrubbed and shining, his hair smooth and wet, was ready in no time. Proudly he climbed into the seat beside Miss Bird. Sitting very straight and smiling happily, he waved goodbye, and off rolled the little van, starting on another busy day.

"Amanda isn't home," said Pyxie as the car took them past the Barrs' front yard lying strangely quiet in the morning sun. "She and Thanny have gone to the shore, to their aunt's. She lives right by the ocean, Amanda says."

"Amanda and Thanny must be having fun." Miss Bird glanced down at Pyxie's happy face. "But I like it here in the country, too. Don't you?"

Indeed, it was pleasant rolling along the summer road, with the sky so blue above them and the bright sun shining overhead. The fresh wind, touched with the sea not far away, blew in their faces, bringing them a faint sting of salt air mingled with the odor of the pines and the wayside flowers. The flat, sandy road of southern New Jersey unwound like a ribbon before them. Birds and squirrels and a rabbit, here and there, flickered and darted among the pines and scrub oak trees that lined the way.

Now and then they passed great stretches of woodland that had been swept by forest fire. Gaunt and bare, pitiful in their ruin, stood the blackened trees, skeletons of what they once had been, rising from ground burned smooth and brown or standing amid the fresh green of a new undergrowth. Too often they saw the stone foundations of houses destroyed by the blaze that spreads so rapidly in hot, dry weather, especially if fanned by an untoward breeze.

On rolled the car past the low, dark tangle of cranberry bogs, with the rough houses of the pickers standing nearby.

There were not many large farms, for here the soil was sandy. But wherever they went, hens and chickens and turkeys were to be both heard and seen. Hens clucked and scolded their chicks in motherly fashion from the shelter of the fence. Roosters lifted their voices proudly in loud crowing. And excited turkeys darted awkwardly and aimlessly across the road at the risk of their lives.

"You will want to hop out here and walk about," said Miss Bird as she turned in at a wide gateway. "This is a turkey farm."

And Pyxie, escorted by the farmer, spent a happy time among the speckled, gobbling fowl, while Miss Bird carried in an armful of books to the farmer's wife and admired the baby's new tooth.

Wherever she stopped, the Library Lady was made welcome, and in each house she left pleasure behind her in the shape of a book.

Noon found them near a little river. And away from the road, in the shade of the alders and swamp maples, among the cool green of the pussy willows and blackberry vines, they sat down by the narrow brown stream to eat.

"Are you hungry?" asked Miss Bird as she opened the packages and spread their contents upon the ground.

"Yes, ma'am. It makes you hungry to ride 'round and give out books," answered Pyxie with the air of having done most of the morning's work. He eyed with relish his share of the feast and announced, "It's a berry pie. They are the best of all."

So while the little river rippled gently by and the wind blew softly and the sun tried to peep at them through the leaves, the two friends sat and ate and talked together.

Pyxie, reminded of Jenny by the woods about him, told of the happy days they had so often spent wandering out-of-doors together. He was proud, too, to point out to his friend the many different birds he knew.

Then it was time to go, and off they rode again, sometimes rolling swiftly along the highway, sometimes creeping in and out of lonely, sandy little crossroads and lanes. When the houses were far apart, Miss Bird drove into the yard and left her books at the door. In a village or tiny hamlet, all the books of the neighborhood were carried into one place; it might be a house or a store. Then Pyxie was able to help, and he gladly ran back and forth with load after load.

It was growing cooler now. Evening was coming on.

"This is the last place we stop," said Miss Bird, bringing the van to a standstill before a small, gray house with nasturtiums blazing along the garden walk. "Grandpa and Grandma Morton live here. There is Grandma now."

A plump little woman stepped out on the side porch, a pleasant little old woman with white hair and shining gold spectacles that couldn't hide the twinkle in her bright blue eyes.

She waved a greeting and looked curiously at Pyxie, who, in shyness, turned his head away.

"Who is the little boy with you, Miss Bird?" she inquired. "Is he your brother? I don't get a speck of news living 'way back here in the country the way I do."

Miss Bird laughed as she and Pyxie stepped down from the van.

"His name is Pyxie Earl," she answered. "He is my friend. He wants to stretch his legs and have a drink of water at the well."

"Wait! He must have a doughnut, too." Grandma Morton hurried indoors and came back with a plate of sugary doughnuts. "Help yourselves, both of you. Do!

Now, you run out to the barn, boy," she said. "Grandpa is out there, and he has something that you would like to see. Miss Bird, I hope you have brought me a lively book to read. I'd like one with lots going on."

While Grandma Morton and Miss Bird were choosing a lively book, Pyxie made his way to the barn and stood looking shyly in at the open door.

Grandpa Morton, as tall and thin as Grandma was short and plump, spied the little figure and beckoned him in.

"Come in, son," he said. "Miss Bird bring you? Look what I have here in this stall."

Pyxie looked, just one look. Then down he went on his knees in the straw. For there, in the stall, were four little puppies, tumbling and crawling about—four little brown puppies with trustful brown eyes and soft, silky hair and absurd little tails that wagged and thumped the straw as if Pyxie were an old and dear friend.

"Do you like them?" Grandpa Morton sat down on an overturned pail and gently poked the nearest puppy in the ribs with a big forefinger. "I'm giving them away. Would you like to take one home with you? Would you like to have one to keep?"

"I don't know whether Miss Mattie would let me have a dog."

That was all Pyxie said. But his face showed what he felt. It said, as plainly as words, that he would rather have one of these little dogs than anything else in the whole wide world.

He put out his hand and patted one of the puppies who had rested his paws on the little boy's knee and was looking inquiringly into his face.

"I don't know whether Miss Mattie would let me have a dog," he said again.

"Maybe she would." Grandpa sounded hopeful. "Here is Miss Bird. Let's ask her and see what she thinks."

"Suppose we take a puppy home and ask Miss Mattie," was Miss Bird's answer. Her keen eyes had seen the longing look on Pyxie's face. "If she doesn't want to keep him, I will bring him back myself."

"Which one do you want?" asked Grandpa.

Pyxie didn't have to stop to think.

"This one," he said, pointing to the puppy who was still snuggled up against his knee. "I like him best because he likes me."

Seated in the car with the puppy in his arms, Pyxie's happy face smiled goodbye to Grandpa and Grandma Morton, who were calling their farewells from the little side porch.

Out on the road, moving swiftly toward home, he glanced up now and then at Miss Bird. But most of the time he kept his eyes fixed on the silky brown head, the cold black nose, and the soft forepaws of his new friend, lying contentedly on his knees. The car rolled smoothly along, and presently the brown eyes closed and, with a long, gentle sigh, the little dog fell asleep.

"Miss Bird," said Pyxie in a hushed voice, "do you know what I am going to name my dog, if Miss Mattie lets me keep him?"

Miss Bird shook her head.

"I am going to call him Daniel Boone," said Pyxie. "I think that is a good name, don't you?"

He looked fondly down at the brown head on his knee. He bent and whispered in the silky, sleeping ear.

"Your name is Daniel Boone," whispered Pyxie. "Do you like that name? I do."

Chapter 10

Daniel Boone

The moment Miss Mattie saw Daniel Boone, she liked him.

Perhaps that was because he tried to climb into her lap and kiss her hand with his rough little tongue. Perhaps it was because she couldn't help laughing whenever he wagged his funny, stubby little tail. Perhaps—and this was most likely the real reason—it was because she saw that Pyxie had set his heart upon keeping the little dog, and so she wanted to like him, too.

But whatever the reason, Daniel Boone stayed.

That first evening, Miss Mattie and Pyxie stood over him and watched him hungrily eat his supper of milk with a little bread broken through it. They made a soft bed for him in a box out in the woodshed and together tucked him under the old green shawl that was to keep him comfortable and warm. When he cried and whined in the night, which of course he did because he was lonely and homesick for his mother and brothers and sisters back in Grandpa Morton's barn, it was Miss Mattie who went down to the woodshed and comforted Daniel Boone until he fell asleep again. She told Pyxie about it in the morning, for Pyxie had slept through it all and hadn't heard a sound.

The little dog was great company, for Pyxie had missed Amanda and Thanny, who were still visiting their aunt at the shore. But now he had someone who was always ready to romp and play with him—someone who would gladly, if he could, follow at his heels wherever he went, and who welcomed him home again after an absence with loud barking and frantic wagging of an eager little tail.

Daniel Boone's heart was large enough to take in Miss Mattie, too. Every morning he greeted her at the kitchen door with sharp little barks. In the evening, on the porch steps, when it began to grow dark, he liked to snuggle confidingly against her side. These attentions amused and pleased Miss Mattie. She thought it good, too, for Pyxie to have the care and training of this playmate and pet.

"I'm real glad you brought him home," she said as she watched the little boy try to teach his friend to sit up and beg. This was a lesson that began in earnest, but which usually ended in a roll and tumble on the floor. "You think more of your own manners now that you have to teach them to somebody else."

There was one member of the family, however, who was not fond of Daniel Boone. James, waddling about his pen, peering over the side, never failed to snap suddenly out at the little silky-brown newcomer, who nimbly managed to keep out of reach of the yellow bill and who answered James' hisses with barks sharp and shrill.

"It's good we had the extra board put 'round James' pen to make it high," said Pyxie as the sound of mingled hisses and barks came from back of the house. "I am glad he can't get out. I don't know what would happen if he caught hold of Daniel Boone."

"Poor James! I believe he is jealous," said kind-hearted Miss Mattie. "We must give him something extra for supper tonight. It doesn't do to neglect old friends for new."

Now, of course Daniel Boone was young, very young. Everyone understood that. No one expected him to have more sense than most little puppies can boast. Miss Mattie well knew that puppies like a plaything that they can chew and worry to their hearts' content. So she gave Daniel Boone an old shoe, one of her own, which he kept in his bed, buried under his shawl, and in which he took great comfort and pleasure, too.

If Daniel Boone had been content to shake and drag and worry the old shoe, and nothing else, both Pyxie and Miss Mattie would have been spared a great deal of worry, not to mention hard work.

But, after all, Daniel Boone didn't know any better. And it really, in a way, was no one's fault. Though, of course, if Pyxie had kept his eye on the puppy, instead of forgetting all about him, it could never have happened.

It was one Monday morning, and Miss Mattie was busy washing clothes at the tub that stood on the back kitchen porch. The clothesline was stretched from pole to pole at the side of the house in the sun, and as fast as Miss Mattie washed a tubful, she stepped out and hung the clothes up to dry.

Pyxie was sitting in the cellarway on the other side of the house. Miss Mattie's toolbox stood before him, and he was happily sorting nails and screws and odds and ends.

The day was hot and still. Locusts sang in the trees. There was no air stirring.

Suddenly, in the quiet, Pyxie heard a cry.

"Oh! Oh! Daniel Boone, you let go!"

It was Miss Mattie's voice. There was trouble of some kind. Pyxie could tell.

Dropping his nails, he ran as fast as he could around the house.

There, under the clothesline, stood Daniel Boone, in playful mood, a gay, roguish light in his eye. In his mouth he held a corner of the red-and-white kitchen tablecloth, washed and hung on the line to dry. He was pulling and worrying and jerking it with all his strength, running and jumping merrily to and fro. From one corner he had already torn a large piece that lay sadly in the grass, and his sharp little teeth were making a hole in the end he now held.

The red-and-white tablecloth! The very cloth from which Pyxie ate all his meals. Why, it belonged to Miss Mattie! Pyxie could scarcely believe that even Daniel

Boone would harm Miss Mattie's property, and in such a senseless way.

Miss Mattie was running to save the tablecloth. Pyxie ran, too, to pull it from Daniel Boone's eager mouth.

But they were too late. The damage was done, and before their eyes. In the midst of the pulling and jerking, with a loud, shrieking sound, the tablecloth tore in two. There it hung—a ruin.

Encouraged by this feat, with a mighty tug, Daniel Boone pulled half of it from the line and proceeded to shake it vigorously about over the grass. The other half of the tablecloth remained on the line, drooping dismally, a great piece gone from one corner, too.

The tablecloth was ruined forever. Even Pyxie knew that. It could never be used again.

Pyxie stared aghast at the sight. He stood still as if rooted to the ground, while Miss Mattie, looking very sober, took from the line what was left of the tablecloth and slowly folded it into a square.

No one spoke. It was very quiet. The only sound was that made by Daniel Boone as he trailed the tablecloth

round and round and at last twisted himself in it and lay panting in the tangle on the grass.

"Here, you! Give me that!"

Pyxie pulled the forlorn strip of red and white from between Daniel Boone's flapping, waving paws.

"I'll take it, Pyxie." Miss Mattie spoke quietly at his side. "Don't you hit Daniel Boone. He's only a little dog. You go tie him up in the woodshed so he will know he's done wrong."

And Miss Mattie, bearing the two strips of tablecloth, went back to her washtub, leaving Pyxie to tie Daniel Boone in the woodshed, where he promptly rolled himself into a ball and went to sleep before Pyxie could explain to him what a dreadful thing he had done.

"Miss Mattie," began Pyxie solemnly when they sat down at noon to a table, which, though scoured white, looked strange without the familiar red-and-white cover—"Miss Mattie, how much does a red-and-white tablecover cost?"

"Cost?" Miss Mattie stared for a moment. "A new one, you mean? Oh, about a dollar, I should say. Maybe a little more."

"A dollar? That's a hundred cents. That's four quarters, isn't it?"

And Pyxie's face grew sober. The sum seemed a large one to him.

"The tablecloth wasn't new, Pyxie," said Miss Mattie. "Don't you worry about it one bit. It was old. That's why it tore. But I liked it. And it made me feel kind of sorry to see it go."

"Yes, ma'am. I feel sorry, too," was Pyxie's answer. "And, maybe, by and by, I can make Daniel Boone feel sorry about it. He ought to. He's the one that spoiled it all."

Miss Mattie laughed a little at this.

"Don't think any more about it," she advised. "We can get along without a tablecloth for a while, I guess."

But Pyxie did think about it. That afternoon he sat for a long time, his elbows on his knees, his chin in his hands. Then he went into the woodshed, where Daniel Boone still lay in lonely disgrace.

Pyxie's voice could be heard in earnest talk, with now and then a short bark or whine from the perplexed

Now and then a short bark or whine from the perplexed Daniel Boone

Daniel Boone, who had no idea why he must stay in the woodshed as if it were night instead of romping with his playfellow or dozing in the sun.

Presently Pyxie came out of the woodshed. He walked straight through the yard out to the road, where he set off, in a determined fashion, without once looking back, as if he knew just where he meant to go.

It was almost suppertime before Miss Mattie discovered that Pyxie was gone. She called, and there was no answer. She waited, and he did not come. She searched, and he was not to be found.

Daniel Boone eyed Miss Mattie anxiously. He whined a little and barked. When she untied him, he searched, too, but in aimless puppy fashion; and after his supper, he curled up in his bed and went to sleep.

Miss Mattie was not so carefree. She couldn't eat her supper, though she tried. She sat watching the road till dusk fell. Then, her forehead puckered with worry, she made her way over to the Barrs' and found them alone on their front steps.

"It isn't a bit like him to act this way," said Miss Mattie when she had told how Pyxie had gone without a word and had not come home yet. "He has always been a real good boy. I can't understand where he is."

"He has gone fishing and forgot to come home," said Mr. Barr easily. "He'll be along directly—you'll see."

"The best children are dreadfully thoughtless at times," contributed Mrs. Barr, thinking of some of Amanda's pranks. "I believe Mr. Barr is about right. He'll come. Don't fret."

"But it isn't a bit like him," repeated Miss Mattie. "He wouldn't forget to come home. He's a real steady, dependable little boy."

Miss Mattie's face was so filled with distress that Mr. Barr, after thinking it over, slowly rose to his feet.

"What say, Miss Mattie, if you and I go down to the woods where Pyxie came from and look 'round a little," he said. "I'll take a lantern, and we can go in and call and shout. Mother, you had better stay here and watch the road."

Miss Mattie had started down the steps before Mr. Barr finished his speech. She longed to be searching, to be doing something, to be going somewhere. Anything was better than sitting still.

But just before the search party set out, Miss Mattie seized Mrs. Barr's arm and gave it an excited shake.

"Look there, at the road!" exclaimed Miss Mattie. "Isn't that a little boy coming along all alone?"

Without waiting for an answer, she hurried down the path, followed by Mr. and Mrs. Barr. There, in the summer dust, they waited for him—waited for Pyxie, who came trudging slowly along the dusty road.

"Where have you been?" called out Miss Mattie in a voice that quavered a little. "Where on earth have you been all this time?"

"You've worried Miss Mattie 'most to death," began Mrs. Barr sharply. "I don't know but I should give you a good whipping if you belonged to me."

Pyxie looked from face to face. Then he spoke out.

"I've been working," said Pyxie. "I've earned fifteen cents." He held out his hand, and they could see the glitter of the coins in the dark. "It's for your tablecloth, Miss Mattie. We're going to buy a new one when I have money enough."

"For pity's sake!" Miss Mattie lifted her hands helplessly and let them fall.

For a moment she couldn't speak. Then she turned to the Barrs to explain what Pyxie meant.

"His dog tore up my tablecloth today," she began feebly, "and if he isn't out, earning money to buy a new one!"

Then Miss Mattie gathered herself together. She grasped Pyxie by the arm.

"Who gave you that money?" she demanded. "Where have you been to work?"

"I've been up the back road, where I used to live," answered Pyxie. He seemed surprised at the excitement he had caused. "Tony has a vegetable farm back up in there. I've been picking beans for him, and he gave me the fifteen cents. I'm going back tomorrow. He wants me. He will give me fifty cents if I work all day."

"It's miles off," said Miss Mattie hotly. "You shan't go a step."

"Please, Miss Mattie. I have to go," said Pyxie earnestly. "I said I would. It isn't so far. I must go two days more, anyway, till I have enough to buy a new tablecloth. It was my dog that tore it up."

Pyxie turned to Mr. Barr as if he felt that a man would understand what he was doing and why. A man would know what was just and right. Their eyes met in a long look, and Mr. Barr spoke a word for the little boy.

"Pyxie is right, Miss Mattie," he said. "His dog did the damage, and he wants to make it good. It isn't so far up to the truck farm. You let him go."

Miss Mattie did not commit herself. She put her arm around Pyxie's shoulders and drew him close. She saw before her a tired, hungry little boy.

"You come home now to supper and bed," she said. "We'll talk about truck farms in the morning. But why didn't you tell me you were going? What made you walk off without saying a word?"

"I'm sorry I didn't tell you, Miss Mattie. It was because I knew you wouldn't let me go," answered Pyxie. "That's why. Here is the money, Miss Mattie. You keep it. It's fifteen cents. How's Daniel Boone? Did he miss me? Is he all right?"

In the morning, Pyxie went back to the truck farm.

"I've been thinking it over," said Miss Mattie, "and I see you are right. Daniel Boone is your dog, and if he does damage, as Mr. Barr says, you want to make good. But I've been thinking this, too, Pyxie. It's the kind of a thing that Lindbergh and George Washington and King Arthur would have done when they were little boys. And I am glad enough that you are turning out to be that kind."

Pyxie brightened at this encouragement. He tucked a large parcel of lunch under his arm and bade a tender farewell to Daniel Boone, who somehow had grown more dear now that Pyxie was paying the price of his innocent mischief.

He started off briskly on his long walk to the vegetable farm, hidden back among the pines and owned by a thrifty Italian who knew Pyxie's story and was glad of his help at this busy time of year.

Pyxie pleased Tony by the way in which he fell to work stripping the bean vines. He did his share all day long, and at five o'clock had well earned the fifty cents which had been promised him.

Curiously enough, on the way home, when Pyxie's steps were beginning to lag, along came Mr. Barr in his shabby, rattling little car. His work had taken him up that way, he said, and he was able to give Pyxie a lift toward home.

"You shan't go but one day more," declared Miss Mattie as she and Daniel Boone welcomed him from the doorstep. "We are too lonely without you, Daniel Boone and I. A dollar and fifteen cents ought to buy a fine tablecloth. You'll see it will."

And so it did.

With the precious, hard-earned money safely tucked in Miss Mattie's purse, she and Pyxie were driven by Mr. and Mrs. Barr into town. There Pyxie and Miss Mattie spent a long, long time selecting a tablecover that not only looked like the old one, but was also a trifle different so that they might feel they had something new.

"It is like the old one," said Pyxie happily, for at least the tenth time, as they rode homeward, the new tablecover clasped in his hands. "It has the same red-and-white squares, but the flowers running 'round the edge are different. I think it was the prettiest one in the store. Don't you?"

"Yes, I do," agreed Miss Mattie. "And you be sure to tie Daniel Boone in the woodshed next washday when it is on the line."

Chapter 11

The Cranberry Pickers

It was the first of September, and as yet there was scarcely a hint of autumn in the air. To be sure, the goldenrod waved its bright sprays along the roadside, and the grapes were beginning to show the faintest rosy and purple bloom. But the cottage gardens were gay with hosts of flowers, the leaves on the trees hung thick and green, and morning after morning dawned warm and summerlike and fair.

Below the roadside stretched the low cranberry bogs, marked off with ditches, narrow and straight. There they lay, a tangle of vines, with their small evergreen leaves, dark and shining, and their glossy red berries, plump now and ripe and ready to be picked.

Pyxie, in his blue overalls, his hair flying, and Daniel Boone, barking at his heels, came running along the road. Pyxie stopped and climbed upon the fence to look down into the bog. The narrow little stream nearby meandered along, looking deep and cool under the old wooden bridge.

"It's pretty this morning," he said, thinking to himself that the sunshine made the dew look like little silver stars. "My! See the mosquitoes! They're thick today."

And Pyxie slapped vigorously and whirled his arms about to drive away the cloud of mosquitoes and flies that came swarming hungrily out of the bog.

"Come on, Daniel Boone. I'll show you where the pickers live."

With the puppy racing on ahead, Pyxie made his way across the road where stood a rough wooden building that looked more like a barn than a house. The doorway stood open, for it had no door, and the windows were only square holes cut here and there.

Daniel Boone sniffed curiously at a pile of smoke-blackened stones lying near the house.

"Come in the house with me," ordered Pyxie. "You keep away from that heap of stones. That is where the pickers cooked last year. Amanda said so. It's the way the gypsies do, Miss Mattie read me, cooking out-of-doors."

Once over the high doorsill, Pyxie studied with interest the two rooms, one on either side of the door. They were empty but for two huge double-decked beds, filled with straw. Pyxie had never seen beds like them before.

"Do you see, Daniel Boone?" mused Pyxie thoughtfully. "Some of the pickers sleep here in this bed, and some of them climb up and sleep in that other one, right over their heads. There must be a lot of people to fill them, they are so big. I'd like to go upstairs, but the steps are all broken down. We had better go outdoors, I guess."

Across the lane from the house stood a row of sheds, open on one side and strewn like the beds with straw. Daniel Boone ran gaily toward them. There was no telling what doggy treasure he might find buried in their midst. But Pyxie sternly called him away.

"That is only where some of the men pickers sleep," Pyxie told him with all the wisdom a little boy may show to his dog. "Amanda said so. Don't you see the straw they lie on? There is nothing there for you."

Back on the road again, Pyxie hesitated a moment and then cautiously climbed down into the bog. He wanted to see how nearly ripe the cranberries had grown. From the roadway, the more timid Daniel Boone watched his master anxiously, his brown eyes following every move. He barked joyously and whirled around after his own tail when Pyxie was safe at his side once more.

"The pickers will be here soon," reported Pyxie, "for the cranberries are ripe. They are as red as red can be."

It was not surprising, then, that the very next day Pyxie ran in to Miss Mattie with a piece of news.

"The pickers have come!" Pyxie's eyes were bright with excitement. "There are ever so many of them. The house and the sheds are full. I saw some boys like me, and some girls, and there are babies, too."

"Are they Italians?" asked Miss Mattie, looking up from her work. "Did you say a good many came this time?"

Miss Mattie was used to the yearly visit of the pickers. Every fall, when the cranberry crop was ripe, she had seen them come from their homes in the city or from the farms where they had been gathering the fruits and vegetables in season. And once the cranberries were picked, off they would go again, old and young, babies and bundles, to another piece of work.

"I think they are Italians. Most of them have black hair, and they talk very fast," said Pyxie, somewhat in doubt. "I am going back to see them again, and I'll try to find out. I'll count them, too, if I can."

The cranberry bogs where the pickers were to work were not very large, as bogs go. And the corps of pickers was small as compared with certain great bogs just across the county line, where a large number of pickers were well cared for in comfortable homes.

But to Pyxie, peering out from behind a bush, there seemed no end to the people moving in and out and about the house and sheds, and he gave up trying to count them before he had reached ten.

He watched the stout, swarthy women move about their tasks, their golden earrings glittering and swinging as they walked. The women lifted the heavy bundles left lying in the grass and carried them indoors upon their heads as if

There seemed to be no end to the people moving in and out.

they were no heavier than a feather. The men lay dozing on the ground or talked vehemently to one another with flashing eyes and waving arms and hands.

The boys and girls ran noisily about at play among the trees. They were confident and bold, and Pyxie hid behind his bush whenever they looked his way. He did not think he would like to play with them.

Something, a movement or a sound, made Pyxie jump and look behind him.

There stood a little boy, a little Italian boy, gay in a pair of bright green trousers and laughing into Pyxie's startled face.

"You play?" whispered the little boy, as if he would like to join in the game. "You hide? I play, too."

He was a very small boy with lively, dark eyes set in a round, plump face. His mop of dark, curly hair was brushed straight up off his forehead, which gave him a comical look of surprise.

"I play, too," said the little boy again, and he knelt down at Pyxie's side behind the bush.

"I wasn't playing," explained Pyxie. "I was watching the folks that have just come."

"They are my folks." The little boy seemed pleased to own them. "I'm Joe. I whistle."

He pursed up his lips and, in spite of his size, broke forth into a whistle as clear and as tuneful as a bird's.

It was a bright and lively little air he was trilling, and Pyxie liked it. He liked Joe, too, so friendly and funny and gay.

"My father." Joe pointed to a man who had crossed the road and was looking down into the cranberry bog. "His name is Louis. He's the Boss. He tells everybody what to do."

"You mean he bosses the pickers?" Pyxie eyed Louis with great respect.

Joe nodded.

"I pick, too," he added proudly. "We all pick. We make the money. See my mother, in the doorway." Joe pointed to a pretty little woman in a bright pink dress. "See, she goes to speak to Anita. Anita cooks. She cooks for us all."

Anita was a brown, withered little old woman. The gold hoops in her ears sparkled as she stirred with a long spoon a potful cooking over a fire on the heap of stones. She kept a watchful eye upon the half dozen babies who slept or crawled about in the grass.

"We eat now." Joe's mother and Old Anita were filling a huge pile of plates with macaroni from the pot. The other women and the big girls were carrying the platefuls to the men. Pyxie smelled coffee. He saw great plates heaped with crusty bread. The boys and girls came running from the woods.

"I go now," said Joe, his eyes on the pot and spoon. "You come back by an' by?"

With a friendly smile, Joe waited for Pyxie's nod. Then, bravely whistling his tune, off he ran, his bright green legs twinkling over the grass.

Pyxie slipped away home. He told Miss Mattie all he had seen. He told her about Joe, too.

"He is a little boy, but he knows how to whistle," said Pyxie, with pride in his new friend. "He's funny. He laughs, and he makes me laugh, too. I like him."

The next morning, Pyxie made his way back to the cranberry bog. The pickers were at work. Men and women and children were in their places down in the bog, picking cranberries by hand as fast as they could. There was little Joe. Pyxie spied his bright green trousers. His dark head was bent low over the vines. Louis the Boss moved about here and there, speaking to this one and that. The women made bright spots of color in the dark bog with their waists and skirts of pink and purple, yellow and blue.

Old Anita had been left in charge of the babies. They crept and scrambled about in the grass or peacefully slept while she half dozed in the sun.

Pyxie leaned on the fence and watched the pickers.

"Hi! Boy!"

Pyxie didn't answer. He didn't think that anyone was calling to him.

Presently he heard the voice at his side and felt a touch on his arm. It was Louis, smiling at him and showing a row of strong, white teeth.

"You want to work?" asked Louis. "You want to make fifty, seventy-five cent' every day? You come on and work. You come on with me."

"I'll have to ask," said Pyxie in doubt. "I don't know whether I can or not."

"Not too much pickers," explained Louis, waving his hand toward the bog. "Two men sick. They no come now. They come by an' by. You go ask. You come work. Seventy-five cent' every day, you tell."

Pyxie rushed home. He darted in upon Miss Mattie, tripping over Daniel Boone, who leaped out of the way with a frightened yelp.

"I can earn some money!" gasped Pyxie, red-faced and panting. "The man wants me to come pick in the cranberry bog. He will give me seventy-five cents a day. Can't I go? I said I would come and ask."

Miss Mattie looked at Pyxie over her spectacles. She put on a disapproving air.

"It is too hot down in the bog," she objected. "The mosquitoes are as big as hawks, and they don't give you a minute's peace. You don't need money for anything, Pyxie. I guess you had better keep out of that."

"I want to do it." Pyxie's face showed his disappointment. "I want to go pick in the bog."

"Amanda will be home in a few days," said Miss Mattie, "and school will open before you know it. You had better play and have a good time while you can."

"Let me pick till Amanda comes home," pleaded Pyxie. "Then I'll stop, and I won't ask again. I truly won't."

"Well," Miss Mattie unwillingly yielded, "it won't do any harm, I suppose. Maybe, after one day of it, you will be glad to stop."

Pyxie waited for no further permission. In a twinkling, he was back at the cranberry bog and found himself, basket in hand, down among the vines, picking away as fast as he could, like his neighbors all roundabout.

Miss Mattie was quite right about the mosquitoes. They hummed, they sang, they tickled. Above all, they bit.

But Pyxie didn't mind. Louis had put him next to lively little Joe, and he was glad to be there. He carried his basket proudly. He meant to work hard and do well.

Joe, his face hot, his black curls standing out, smiled and nodded at sight of his friend of yesterday.

"Hello! You come pick, too?" he said, his little brown fingers flying.

Pyxie soon caught the knack of stripping the cranberries from the thick and tangled vines. He worked on in silence, as busy as his neighbor, and the mound in his basket grew higher and higher.

Joe began to whistle. He knew more than one tune. As Pyxie listened to the trills and quavers, he found himself smiling. The berries seemed to come faster, too.

The little girl on Pyxie's other hand smiled when she heard the music. Her name was Philomena. She was a slow worker, and Louis, every now and then, had to urge her to hurry.

Louis moved off to the other side of the bog, and Joe allowed himself to talk a little to his friend.

"Can you whistle?" inquired Joe, trilling like a blackbird to show what he could do.

"No, but I can read," was Pyxie's reply.

Joe shook his head.

"Not me," he said with a careless air. "I don't go to school much. Only in winter, when it's cold."

Pyxie started at this. He wanted to know why.

"We go pick on different farms. But not wintertime. Wintertime we stay home," Joe told him, shrugging his shoulders as he had seen his father do. "We pick strawberries, raspberries, vegetables. We just picked blackberries. They're all gone. Now the cranberries come."

Pyxie ran back in the afternoon, eager to work again. He and Joe exchanged smiles. They whispered a little when Louis was not near. By the time five o'clock came, Pyxie felt that he had made a new friend.

In the evening after supper, Pyxie and Daniel Boone had an old-time roll and tumble on the grass.

"I've worked all day," confided Pyxie in the puppy's silken ear, "and now I want some fun."

Daniel Boone was very willing. He had missed his playfellow and felt himself a trifle neglected. He jumped and tumbled and barked in an ecstasy of pleasure.

When Miss Mattie came out on the steps, he lost his head completely and rushed at her and barked as if she were a stranger he had never seen before.

"There! There! That will do," she said, so soothingly that Daniel Boone came to his senses and sheepishly snuggled up against her side with his nose in her lap.

Pyxie, on the step below, was thinking of his day in the cranberry bog and of lively Joe.

"Every night Joe's father plays the 'mandolin' and Joe whistles," announced Pyxie. "He knows lots of tunes. He wants me to go hear him sometime."

"You mustn't go without asking," said Miss Mattie absently, her eyes on the treetops.

"I put my money in the blue teapot on the shelf," went on Pyxie. "I'm going to earn more money. I'm going to buy you a watch or maybe a collar for Daniel Boone."

"You are only going to pick two days more," was Miss Mattie's answer to this. "Amanda will be home day after tomorrow. Her mother went down to the shore today to bring the children home."

"I like to pick." Pyxie surveyed his scratched fingers and his mosquito bites with pride. "I like Joe, too. He makes me laugh. I wish you could see his green trousers, Miss Mattie. The boys 'round here don't wear them like that."

Suddenly, a glare sprang up in the sky, and Miss Mattie caught her breath.

"See that light!" she exclaimed. "I'm dreadfully afraid that means a fire in the woods somewhere. We haven't had rain for a month. It's a mercy there is no wind."

But the blaze in the sky died down. And Miss Mattie and Pyxie and Daniel Boone went to bed and slept so soundly that not even the shrill concert of the crickets under the apple tree could disturb their rest.

Chapter 12

Forest Fire

The next day, working in the cranberry bog, Pyxie smelled smoke. A light pearly-gray haze filled the air, though the hot sun steadily blazed its way across a blue and cloudless sky.

A truckload of tired men, their faces grimed with smoke, rolled past the bog. They were firefighters on their way home after a night's work of beating flaming underbrush.

At noon Miss Mattie told Pyxie that fire had broken out in the woods beyond the village of Little Turkey, six miles away.

"Mr. Barr has been called out by the fire warden to help fight it," she said. "I only hope the wind won't rise."

As the afternoon wore on, the haze grew more dense. The sun hung, like a copper coin, in a thick, yellow sky.

The pickers worked slowly. The heat made them languid. Only lively Joe seemed not to mind the hot sun and the mosquitoes. He whistled his gay little tunes under his breath and grinned cheerfully every time Pyxie looked his way. Louis walked round and round the bog, urging the pickers to keep at work, to hurry.

Then Philomena, at Pyxie's side, upset her basket. The cranberries sank down among the tangle of vines into the sand below.

She gave Pyxie a piteous look and began to gather up in her little scratched, brown hands what berries she could. There were tears in her eyes. Her face twisted as if she were going to cry.

Pyxie felt sorry for her.

"Don't you care." He moved over close to her side, and Joe crept over, too.

"Here, take some of mine," said Pyxie. With a lavish hand, he robbed his own basket to fill hers up again, and Joe added a handful or two.

Philomena's face cleared.

"Thanks, thanks," she murmured.

But the boys scrambled hastily back to their places. They didn't want anyone to see what they had done.

"She is only a girl," muttered Pyxie. "We ought to help her out."

"She works slow," added Joe with a businesslike air.

Everyone was glad when five o'clock came and they could leave the bog, with its heat and its mosquitoes. Some of the men and boys went down to bathe in the little stream that was used to flood the bog in winter to keep the vines from the frost. But Pyxie ran home.

That evening he and Miss Mattie sat on the steps as usual. Miss Mattie kept a close watch on the sky, and every little while she asked Pyxie if he thought the smell of smoke was any stronger. There was no light flaring through the trees tonight, and fortunately there was no wind stirring. Pyxie was tired. He went to bed early, leaving Miss Mattie alone on the porch.

Pyxie was dreaming. In the dream someone was shaking his arm.

"Look out, you Joe," muttered Pyxie. "You'll spill my berries. Let me alone."

And he flung his arms about to free himself from the hand that held him fast.

He opened his eyes and sat up. It was not Joe. It was Miss Mattie.

She stood beside his bed, and she was shaking him and calling in his ear.

"Wake up, Pyxie, wake up! The fire is coming! Hurry! Put on your clothes."

Half asleep, Pyxie slid out of bed. By the time Miss Mattie had helped him into his overalls, he was wide awake.

"Where is the fire?" asked Pyxie as Miss Mattie, her fingers clumsy for once, fumbled with a button. "Will we be burned up? What we going to do?"

"We shan't be burned," Miss Mattie spoke briefly. Already she had started down the stairs, Pyxie at her heels.

"Not unless the wind turns. But you never can tell. It's from the south now, strong. It's just come up."

"What are we going to do?" Pyxie repeated his question out in the yard, where the wind was stirring the leaves of the trees and the bushes, and the odor of the flowers came sweet and strong.

"We are going over to the Barrs'. I want him to go wake the pickers. Now the wind has come, they are right in the path of the fire. And it travels fast, I can tell you. If they don't happen to wake up, they are liable to get caught."

Miss Mattie well knew how rapidly a forest fire can travel, especially with a strong wind to send it along. She knew, too, the terror of a pine forest ablaze. More than once, she had heard the fierce crackling of the flames. She had seen the tall pines, proud in their beauty and strength, catch fire, flame torch-like, and then die, leaving only charred skeletons pointing at the sky.

"I'm going to get James," said Miss Mattie. "You fetch Daniel Boone. It isn't likely the fire will come our way at all, but you can never be sure."

Pyxie, excited and very wide awake, ran to the woodshed and dragged the sleepy and wondering Daniel Boone from his comfortable bed. Then, struck by a thought, he darted back into the house.

But he was waiting for Miss Mattie as she came around the corner, driving James before her with a stout little switch broken from the lilac bush.

The strange party of four moved through the wet grass and out into the road. Miss Mattie carried a large, soft bundle under her arm. Pyxie held something that gave forth a pleasant jingle with every step.

"What is that noise, Pyxie?" demanded Miss Mattie, looking down at him. "What have you got there in your hands?"

"The blue teapot," was Pyxie's answer. "It has my money in it. I didn't want to leave it behind."

Miss Mattie made a little sound that was almost a laugh.

"We're just alike," she said, "both carrying our treasures along. I've got my six silver spoons stuck inside my waist and Mother's best patchwork quilt under my arm."

James led the procession as they walked rapidly along the road. He stepped out in majestic fashion, his head held high. Daniel Boone trotted obediently close to his master's heels. He felt there was something wrong. His knowing little tail hung limp. He made no side excursions into the bushes in the hope of frightening out a rabbit, as was his wont.

At every few steps, Miss Mattie turned and looked over her shoulder. She was quick to spy a bright red glow that rose in the sky and fell again.

"There! See that! It's coming nearer!" Miss Mattie quickened her steps. "If those pickers don't see it, they will be caught."

Pyxie began to run at her side. He wanted to hurry, too. He was thinking of little Joe, peacefully sleeping, his gay whistling stilled, while the fire crept nearer and nearer, and no one knew.

"I won't know what to do if Mr. Barr isn't home." Miss Mattie had begun to run, too.

"I thought he went to Little Turkey." Pyxie looked up at Miss Mattie with a troubled face.

"Maybe he's come home." Miss Mattie tried to speak hopefully.

"But s'pose he hasn't." Pyxie stood still in the road. Miss Mattie stopped, too, to turn and look at him.

"Here, you take the teapot." Pyxie thrust it into her hands. "I'm going to run and tell the pickers. I'm going to wake up Louis and little Joe."

"Pyxie, come back! You'll be burned! You'll get caught in the fire!"

Miss Mattie's voice was sharp. She reached out after Pyxie, but she was too late. He was running back along the road they had just traveled. He didn't stop to answer Miss Mattie. He didn't even turn his head.

Daniel Boone started after him. Then he stopped and looked back at Miss Mattie. Wasn't she coming? Well, no matter what happened, Daniel Boone meant to stay with Pyxie. The little brown dog set off again and in a moment was running at his master's side.

Miss Mattie stared after them. Then they were out of sight in the dark. She turned and began to run toward Mr. Barr's.

Pyxie's bare feet made a steady sound on the dusty road—pat, pat, pat, pat. He tried to breathe as the big boys did when they raced at school. Daniel Boone's little paws thudded along at his side.

Now he had passed his own house, standing dark and silent and unfamiliar in the night. He kept on and on and on until he had to stand still to rest and catch his breath. Daniel Boone sat down, panting, with his tongue hanging out of his mouth and his brown eyes fixed on Pyxie's face.

Pyxie wished he and Daniel Boone could have a drink. But there was no water near, and, if there had been, he didn't dare stop. He must reach the shack before the fire did. He must waken Louis. He must be sure that no harm came to friendly, smiling little Joe.

He was rested now. Off he started again. The road was dark. There were only trees and bushes here, not a house. Pyxie wouldn't pass a single house on his way to the shack. But he didn't mind that. He didn't mind anything if only Joe wouldn't be burned.

Now he had reached the turn in the road where the Twin Oaks stood. They were two trees that grew close together, almost as if they had a common root.

Pyxie stopped again to rest. His hair was wet. His heart was pounding. But he was afraid to stand still long.

This was the last lap in his journey. Around the turn, along the road a quarter of a mile, and he would reach the cranberry bog and the sleepers in the shack.

But around the turn the wind blew straight in his face. It was harder to breathe. He was tired now, too. He wanted to stop and rest. But not for all the world would he give up when he had come so far.

He pushed on, his head bent, his hands clenched. He had forgotten how the big boys raced. His legs ached. His throat was very dry. Daniel Boone limped along on three legs. He was very tired, too.

Now wood cinders came blowing along on the breeze. They stuck to Pyxie's wet face and hands. Once, Daniel Boone, with cinders in his nose, had to stop and sneeze.

But Pyxie didn't stop even to see what happened to his dog. For through the trees, to the left, he saw a light. And he knew what it meant. Fire in the woods!

"Perhaps they are all awake and up." The thought crossed Pyxie's mind. "Perhaps they see the fire, too. Maybe I don't have to run so fast."

But in spite of this, he kept on, though his heart seemed one great throb. He was coming nearer. He could see the bog and the little bridge. He could see the shack. It was blacker than the darkness. It was quiet. Not a movement, not a sound.

Pyxie pushed on. He had reached the shack, but his task was not done. He stumbled past the heap of cooking stones that still gave off a faint warmth. He began to call.

"Louis!"

His voice made no sound. It was only a gasp.

"Louis! Joe!"

This was better. It sounded like a croak.

He gathered himself together.

"Louis! Fire! Joe!"

Heads were raised in the sheds over the way. The straw rustled as the men stirred and moved and sat up. A man appeared in the doorway of the shack.

"Eh, what? What's that you say?"

"Fire!" called Pyxie in a voice that didn't sound like his own. "See over there, in the woods! The fire is coming! Hurry and get out!"

He could see the shack. It was blacker than the darkness.

The words were scarcely out of his mouth before the shack and the sheds were alive with people running frantically here and there, shouting to one another, pouring out upon the road.

The air was heavy with smoke. The fire in the woods, driven steadily along by the wind, was not so distant now.

Pyxie crept to the roadside, out of the way, and lay down, panting, in the grass. His whole body seemed to throb with the beating of his heart. Daniel Boone found him and snuggled close, his tongue licking Pyxie's cheek, his tail beating against Pyxie's arm.

There was more shouting. Children were crying. Some of the women screamed.

Now the men drove their cars, hidden back among the trees, down to the road. They crowded the women and the children and the bundles into them as best they could.

Pyxie lay still. He didn't want to move. He couldn't even care about Joe. If everyone was awake and leaving, Joe must be safe, too.

The fire was nearer. You could hear a crackling and a low, humming purr. A tall pine back in the woods caught and flared like a huge torch. Pyxie knew he ought to get up and run away. But he couldn't stir. In just a moment he would go.

A car came rattling and swaying along the road.

A voice called, "Pyxie! Where are you? Pyxie Earl!"

It was Mr. Barr. He leaned from his car, peering into the darkness on either side.

Pyxie sat up and called out, "Here I am!"

But there was so much shouting and crying, so much noise from the other cars, that he couldn't be heard.

It was Daniel Boone's shrill barking that brought Mr. Barr, his car left over the way, running to their side.

He lifted Pyxie in his arms.

"Are you hurt?" asked Mr. Barr. "Did you wake the pickers up?"

Pyxie shook his head to one question and nodded yes to the other.

"I didn't see Louis and Joe," he said, holding fast to his friend, glad to find himself in Mr. Barr's strong arms. He could care now whether his friends were safe.

"Louis!" shouted Mr. Barr. Already he was in his car, Pyxie at his side, Daniel Boone clasped tight in the little boy's arms. "Louis! Joe! Where are you?"

"There is Joe!" Pyxie spied his friend sitting on top of a great bundle in a car filled to overflowing with frightened children and excited women who chattered and screamed. Joe, for the moment, had lost his jaunty air, but he leaned forward on his perch and shouted an answer to his father's name.

"Louis has gone to flood the bog," he called, "because of the fire."

Just then Louis came running up.

"You want me?" he asked. "I hear my name. Somebody called?"

"I called you," answered Mr. Barr as his car started down the road. He had to shout to make himself heard. The other cars were starting off, too. "I want you to know that this boy Pyxie saved your lives. He ran a mile all alone to wake you up. If the fire had caught you asleep—"

But the car whirled them on, out of hearing, leaving Louis staring in the middle of the road.

When they reached the turn at Twin Oaks, Mr. Barr spoke to Pyxie.

"Look back, son," he said. "Look at the shack."

The rough old building stood out in a glare brighter than the light of day. The trees and the bushes behind it were ablaze.

"You did a good night's work, Pyxie," said Mr. Barr, looking down with approval into the grimy little face at his side. "You not only saved the pickers, but you've showed what's in you. You've showed everybody 'round these parts that you are a brave boy."

Chapter 13

The Story That Miss Bird Told

School had opened that morning, and Pyxie was very happy.

He sat in his new seat and swung his feet carelessly and looked about the room.

He was happy because at last he was in a class. Miss Grant had put him there that morning. It was William's class, too. And his seat was now across the aisle from the lonely little desk that had been his when he had first come there to school, strange and new.

As he sat there, his thoughts were pleasant.

"I am in a class, my own class," he was saying to himself with satisfaction. "I am going to work hard and keep up with them all. They'll see."

His face, brown in its summer tan, wore a bright and contented look. You would scarcely have known him for the boy who once had been so lonely and resentful and forlorn. He did not feel like that boy anymore. For now he had his own place in school. He was in a class. He had studied hard, and he had proved that he could learn.

There were other reasons why Pyxie felt confident and happy and proud. The story of his bravery on the night of the forest fire had been told throughout the neighborhood, and people had been quick to praise him for his courage and thought for his friends.

The praise was well deserved. For it was thanks to Pyxie that the pickers had escaped unharmed, every one, though the shack and sheds had burned to the ground. Miss Mattie had not found Mr. Barr at home, and he had come only in time to ride out for Pyxie and bring him safely back.

"Then the Lord sent the rain." Miss Mattie always added these words when that point in the story was reached. She could not forget that her little home had been spared. "The firefighters did their part, I know, when they got there, but 'twas the rain that put the fire out."

Far and wide the story spread. Miss Mattie was even stopped on the road and at church to hear words of praise of her "home boy."

Miss Bird made a special trip to Pyxie's house to tell him how proud of him she felt.

"Why, they have heard about it 'way out at Grandpa Morton's," she said. "Grandma Morton has sent you some of her sugary doughnuts because of what you did."

Yes, Pyxie was a happy boy. Even the children in school seemed different to him now. They were more friendly, he thought. And no doubt he was right. They could not call him "'fraid-cat" any longer. Amanda had seen to it that every one of them should know how truly brave Pyxie had proved himself to be.

Now, on the afternoon of this first day back at school, there came the familiar roll of wheels, and through the door, wide open to the soft September day, Pyxie saw the little green van wheel into the yard and come to a standstill under the trees.

A joyous hum arose. "Miss Bird! The Book Lady! She's here!" How delighted everyone was to see her in school again!

"I've books and more books," said Miss Bird when she had greeted them all.

And for a time every child was busy selecting and chattering and looking over his choice.

Pyxie did find time, however, for a private word in Miss Bird's ear.

"I am in a class," whispered Pyxie, "my own class. Miss Mattie is glad. I ran home at noon to tell."

"I am glad, too," was Miss Bird's answer, "as glad as I can be."

"I know it," said Pyxie, sure of his friend.

"Now, a story, a story!" clamored the children when the books were put aside. "Tell us a story, the first one this year."

Miss Bird nodded. Her blue eyes looked smiling and gay. She seemed quite ready to do as they asked.

"Yes, I have a story to tell you," she said, taking her place before them at the front of the room. "It is called 'Denis and His Three Friends.'"

"There was once a castle," began Miss Bird, "a great stone castle that stood high on a pointed hill. In the castle lived the king and the queen, with more courtiers and servants and helpers than one could count. There were gallant gentlemen-in-waiting and beautiful ladies-in-waiting, too. There were brave huntsmen and fine pages, willing maidservants and menservants as well. The kitchen was crowded with frightened scullions who scurried hither and thither to wait upon a proud and haughty cook. There was a learned court doctor, a jolly court barber, and a cross court tailor, too. There were so many people living in the castle that it was really like a little village, only, of course, they were all gathered under one roof.

"At the foot of the pointed hill lay a little town. But everywhere else, as far as the eye could see, stretched the forest, deep and silent and green.

"One morning, the king and his huntsmen rode out of the gate in the high wall built 'round the castle, setting off for a day's hunting in the woods. Perhaps they would bring home deer or a boar. Surely they would have a string of rabbits dangling from their saddle's bow.

"But at night, when the gate swung back to let them in again, all they brought with them was a little boy—a little, frightened boy whom they had found living alone in a hut in the forest.

"'Denis, do you say?' the king had repeated in his great voice when the little boy, lifted before the king by the chief huntsman, had mumbled his name. 'Well, Denis, you are not so large but we can find a corner in the castle for you.'

"So Denis had been brought to the castle. And there he lived, as the king had said, in a corner of the kitchen, which, unlike the hut in the woods, at least was warm and dry.

"But remember this. When Denis left the hut, three little figures stole out after him and followed him straight into his new home. You couldn't have seen them. Denis didn't see them. No one saw them. But they were there, nevertheless.

"Now Denis became a servant of the servants. He waited upon the scullions who waited upon the cook. But though his life was hard, and he was often cuffed and knocked about, still he kept his eyes open, and he learned many, many things.

"Of all that he saw, he thought the queen the most beautiful. And so she was, for her hair was as soft and dark as a raven's wing, her cheeks were rose-red, and her eyes shone bright as stars. Best of all, she had the sweetest smile in the world.

"Of all that Denis longed for, he longed to become a page to the queen. But there was no chance of this. No, never! For the pages were fine, young gentlemen, wearing rich suits of crimson and carrying on their shoulders a ribbon knot of the queen's own colors, crimson and gold.

"Now one day, Denis, a basket on his arm, was on his way to the kitchen garden to dig potatoes. He would give the potatoes to the scullions, who would hand them to the cook, who would serve them that very day, perhaps, at dinner to the king and queen.

"As he trudged along, he looked through the bushes and saw the queen herself, beautiful as the morning, walking among the golden lilies in the garden, with the learned court doctor at her side. She wore a gown of crimson, and at her waist was a knot of her own colors, crimson and gold. That is, they were at her waist one moment, but the next they were lying on the garden path where they had fallen from her gown. Denis saw them there as plainly as could be. The queen and the doctor had moved slowly on. There was no one in sight. Denis made sure of that. He looked all 'round to see.

"Now, Denis longed for that knot of ribbon with all his heart. If he could never be the queen's page, at least he might have her colors to look at in secret and to handle now and then. If once he picked them up, he could slip them into his basket and no one would be the wiser.

"But do not forget the three little figures that had followed Denis from the hut to the castle. They were Denis' three friends.

"One of them now stood at his elbow. There was no telling where he had come from. He was there, that was all—a plain, rugged little figure that you would not have looked at twice. But in spite of that, there was a strength about him that Denis felt, though he didn't see him at all.

"His name was Honesty. And perhaps that will tell you what he did next. He took Denis by the elbow and walked him over to the knot of ribbon. In a twinkling, Denis snatched it up, and then, hand in hand, he and Honesty ran after the queen.

"When he caught up with her, Denis was dreadfully frightened. But since he had kept his eyes open, he knew what to do. He held out the gay knot of ribbon, and he made the queen a bow—a funny, awkward little bow, but the very best that Denis could make. The queen, being a great lady, did not laugh at the funny little bow, though the learned doctor had to turn his head away to cough behind his hand. The queen took the knot of ribbon. She smiled at Denis her lovely smile. And she made him a curtsy that she would make for the king himself.

"Then Denis ran away, back to the potatoes. And the queen and the learned doctor went on with their walk through the rows of tall, golden lilies that swayed and nodded as the queen went by.

"Now, as it happened, Denis was afraid of the cross old court tailor, whose tongue was as sharp as his own needles and pins. He had a habit, too, of snapping his great shears fiercely and promising Denis that he would cut off the ears of any little boy who did not keep out of his way. So when the court tailor called Denis to empty a basket of scraps

The queen took the knot of ribbon.

left from making new suits for the pages, it took all Denis' courage to ask the favor he did.

"'May I have these scraps?' he asked, clutching the basket and standing ready to run.

"'Take them, take them!' answered the tailor gruffly, beginning to snap his great shears. 'But, remember, off with your ears if you get in my way.'

"Denis didn't wait to hear all this. He ran down to his corner of the kitchen, and there he looked over his basket of scraps. For Denis had made up his mind. He was going to make himself a page's suit out of these scraps. Not that anyone would ever see it. Not that he could ever wear it. But make it he would, if he could.

"So night after night, in his corner, Denis worked away at his page's suit. A kind kitchen wench lent him scissors and needle and thread.

"It was very hard work. For, because the scraps were so small, he was forced to put no less than twenty-one pieces in the suit. And, of course, Denis was no tailor. The seams were crooked and the stitches were too big. He made both sleeves for one arm and he sewed the trousers together hind side before.

"It is certain that Denis never could have made his suit if another of his friends had not come to his help. This friend was Perseverance. At first thought, she might seem to be only a good, work-a-day little creature. But, no, that couldn't be. For on her head she wore a sparkling, radiant crown.

"It was Perseverance who pulled the seams straight and took out the big stitches and set them in over again. It was Perseverance who kept Denis at his task when he wanted to give it up and throw his work away. It was thanks to Perseverance that at last the suit was finished, and not a bad fit either, as Denis couldn't help telling himself with pride. And, all the while, Denis hadn't once seen Perseverance. It isn't likely he had even thought of her name.

"It was not long after that Denis was out in the courtyard when the great gate swung back and in rode the huntsmen, home from their day in the forest. With them, trotting wearily, came a fawn—a little fawn whom Denis knew at a glance. He had seen her often in the forest. He had surprised her more than once as she drank from the stream. She had never feared him. She had let him come quite close, for she knew he would not harm her. They were friends.

"Now the little fawn had been caught by the hunters. Perhaps they meant to kill her. Perhaps they would keep her a captive. In any case, the fawn was in misery and distress.

"Denis waited until no one was looking. Then he crept to where the fawn lay, tied, against the wall.

"'When it is night,' whispered Denis, 'I will open the great gate and set you free.'

"So at midnight he led the fawn down to the gate. This was brave of Denis. If he had been caught, he would surely have been beaten. For all he knew, he might have been killed.

"The gate was heavy. The bolts were stiff. Denis never could have moved them alone. But another of his three friends stood there with him. Her name was Friendship, and she had a beautiful face. Together Denis and Friendship pulled and tugged at the bolts and bars. At last the gate creaked open, and out bounded the fawn, lost among the shadows of the tall forest trees.

"Denis didn't have to shut the gate, for in slipped the jolly court barber, glad to find the gate ajar for him. He had been spending a merry evening with his friends in the town below. He was laughing and chuckling to himself as he came.

"Denis hoped the barber hadn't seen him. But he had. He had seen the fawn bound away, too. And being a barber and fond of talking, he told first one and then another, until the story reached the ears of the king and the queen, and they sent for Denis to question him.

"'Why did you set the fawn free?' asked the king.

"He was so magnificent in his purple robe and his golden crown that little Denis trembled before him. He opened his lips, but he couldn't speak.

"Now the queen was wise. She had been watching Denis with her kind, beautiful eyes. And when he couldn't answer, the queen answered for him.

"'It is as plain as day,' she said. 'He did it because he was the fawn's friend. I should like to have such a boy for my page.'

"And surprising as it was to Denis and to everyone else at the court, he actually became the queen's page.

"When he brought out the suit he had made, the suit that he had patched together from twenty-one scraps, the queen said it was beautiful, the most beautiful suit that any of her pages wore. And as he had no knot of ribbon, she took her own colors from her waist and pinned them on his shoulder.

"And so Denis was what he had longed for: to be a page to the queen."

"Miss Bird"—Amanda spoke out of the silence that had fallen at the story's end—"Miss Bird, somehow Denis makes me think of Pyxie."

"Does he?" said Miss Bird, smiling. "He makes me think of him, too."

THE END

More Books from The Good and the Beautiful Library!

Tiger on the Mountain
by Shirley L. Arora

Jade Dragons
by Florence Wightman Rowland

Melissa Across the Fence
by Augusta Huiell Seaman

Redwood Pioneer
by Betty Stirling

www.thegoodandthebeautiful.com